LEAVING

ELVIS

MICHELLE MICHAU-CRAWFORD

LEAVING ELVIS

And Other Stories

UWA PUBLISHING

First published in 2016 by
UWA Publishing
Crawley, Western Australia 6009
www.uwap.uwa.edu.au

UWAP is an imprint of UWA Publishing,
a division of The University of Western Australia.

THE UNIVERSITY OF
WESTERN
AUSTRALIA

This book is copyright. Apart from any fair dealing for the purpose of private study, research, criticism or review, as permitted under the *Copyright Act 1968*, no part may be reproduced by any process without written permission. Enquiries should be made to the publisher.

Copyright © Michelle Michau-Crawford 2016

The moral right of the author has been asserted.

National Library of Australia
Cataloguing-in-Publication entry:
Michau-Crawford, Michelle, author.
Leaving Elvis: and other stories / Michelle Michau-Crawford.
ISBN: 9781742588025 (paperback)
Short stories, Australian.
A823.4

Typeset in Bembo by Lasertype
Printed by Lightning Source

And that is all so long ago. Though when you forget
the last time: most likely it is not the last time.
Luke Davies, from Totem

For those who can never forget

CONTENTS

Getting on *1948*	*1*
Unchained *1956*	*12*
The lie Paul Carmody told Hazel *1960*	*22*
Ned's daughter *1972–73*	*35*
Naming *1974*	*44*
The light *1976*	*55*
Diseased *1980*	*67*
Happy Haven Holiday Park *1992*	*79*
Unsaid *1999*	*88*
Rendezvous *2005*	*99*
Dodgy narratives *2012*	*107*
Leaving Elvis *2013*	*115*
Can of worms *2016*	*127*
Acknowledgements	*142*

1948

Getting on

Len gets a whiff of the blood-sopped sawdust, recoils and stumbles, banging his hip against the solid wooden counter. The screen door taps shut behind him, barely shifting the flies clinging to the outside of the wooden frame. Inside, it is slightly less hot but there is no real respite from the sweltering heat. Righting himself, he grins at David Smith, the town's butcher, and somehow manages to stand tall while leaning on his stick.

'What are you doing here, Len? Middle of the bloody day.'

'What do you think I'm doin', Davo? Came to say g'day.' Len feigns offence and sways slightly. 'Bloody good bloke, your big brother…for a Pommie bastard.' He salutes. 'And you too, of course, are a fine man.'

Len stands at ease. Hums a few lines of 'Mad Dogs and Englishmen'.

'Took Evie to see a Noël Coward revue once, at His Majesty's, up in Perth. Before we were married. Pretty little thing she was.' He taps his cane on the ground a couple of times. 'Had an uncle in the theatrical world. Bit of a nancy, as your big brother, rest his soul, would say. I thought about becoming an actor for a while. Did you know that?'

'Bulldust, Len, you're a farmer through and through.' David points to the door at the side of the counter. 'Go through, mate. I was about to close up and make a cuppa, anyway. Nobody in their right mind wants meat on a scorcher like today.'

In the kitchen at the rear of the butcher's shop, Len takes a seat at the wooden table and sits quietly for a minute or two. He starts talking as David opens up the back door to allow the miserable wisp of breeze through. He'd love another beer but knows Davo won't go for that. Teetotaller from day dot, that one. Too much of his mother's churchy goodness, his brother Joe used to say.

He's not so drunk that he forgets that Davo knows the story he's about to tell. But he likes repeating it. It grows a bit each time – a bit more drama to embellish the facts. And in a way it brings Joe closer. *Never let the truth stand in the way of a good story,* Joe'd laugh when caught out with the bulldust.

'Cracks me up to think of it, even now. Unbelievable how we ended up across the way from one another in the hospital ship.'

Len didn't remember getting out. One minute he was doing what he'd been doing for the past fortnight or so, managing as best he could to hide the fact of his foot swelling and festering, the poison from the rot inching its way through his body, burning like buggery. Then he was flat on his back, swaying in and out of sleep on a hospital ship, with nothing to show for the past few weeks but a thumping headache that consumed his entire body, and a shock of pain where he used to have a foot. Messed with his mind, the poison. Thought he was gunna die. Thought he was already dead. He was scared as hell in his lucid moments, he remembers that much. Not being hot anymore. And feeling that somehow he'd pushed through a new type of evil, and he wasn't burning in all kinds of hell, after all.

Sad and sorry cases, the pair of 'em were. Well, them and the rest of the motley bunch crammed into the hospital ship. Hard to imagine they'd all been in the prime of their lives, him and Joe virile young men with children to prove the fact, just a few months earlier. Now they stank of impending death, and of close shaves, and of narrow escapes from a meeting with The Maker. That, and months of caked-on sweat, shit and fear. The war in Europe had supposedly been done with about three months earlier, and they were half expecting to learn that the victory over Japan was a hoax. Most weren't going to say it out loud after all they'd endured. But they were scared. It was like now they'd got the one thing in life they'd wished for the hardest, and they might wake up and find it snatched away. Some sick bastard's idea of a joke. Worried that they could go down into the blue, they were, too.

In the beginning, Len really didn't know or care that much, one way or the other. But a while into the trip he'd wondered aloud if they'd throw the bodies overboard if they carked it. Wondered what'd happen if the ship arrived – assuming they weren't torpedoed mid-way – emptied of casualties. A ghost ship, sailin' into port.

Nearly fell off his hospital stretcher with the shock of it when Joe spoke up – or cacked and spluttered and just about choked with laughter, more like it. Kept laughing about the fact that they'd started off fighting in different parts of the war, and what do you know, they're now near enough to sharing a room. *Strike me pink. We survived the war. You gunna bloody talk us all to death, Lenny?* They laughed so hard at that. Joe'd said to be sure to tell his missus and kids that if he croaked, he'd died laughing at the irony of the situation. By the time the pigeon-faced old bag of a sister came down between the rows to squawk at 'em to be quiet, they'd established themselves as the Laurel and Hardy of the hospital ship. But they'd protested when someone'd called them that. *No!* they'd called out together, both remembering the film they'd seen at the pictures before going off to war. *Abbott and Costello!* Felt pretty good for them to be laughing, despite the pain. Had half of the banged-up mob on board chortling by then, it seemed.

'Good mates with adjoining properties but never directly crossed paths in the war, the two of us, until they shipped us home. How'd you be?' Len says.

Not that you'd expect to cross paths, not really. It was a big bloody war. Len reminds David of the fact that they'd signed up at different times. Joe early, him late. Funny, to think about it. Shipped back to Australia together, shared a ward in the city hospital for the first couple of weeks, then trundled back here, to the regional hospital. Metal-framed beds with lumpy mattresses lined up on the verandah. A view of the river, they had. Same spot, by his reckoning, that his old man had been laid up after the first one.

He stops talking when his old man comes into his head. His thoughts grow too dark to go on. After going away and seeing something of what a man is capable of doing to another man, he gets that the old bastard might once have been a decent bloke. But it still hurts to think about it. His mother loved his old man once, she'd always maintained that, and was responsible for him, and loyal until the end. But she'd had to hide Len away too often as a kid. She'd give him that look and off he'd go, quiet as a church mouse, to the space between the big old broken cupboard and the wall. Afterwards she'd make all the excuses under the sun for his father's swinging moods, his alternating long blank silences and crazed rages. *He came home alive but not the same*, she'd say, pretending that she could see through her bung eye and that her face wasn't mashed to a pulp, trying to smile at Len as she coaxed him out of the hidey-hole.

He'd never remembered his old man being any different. Didn't really have any happy childhood remembrances. Best thing about his childhood was getting on his pony and riding to school, dawdling as long as he could on the way back. Avoidance of the old bastard, that's what his life was all about for as long as he could remember. But she never blamed him. Bloody saint, his ma was. Kept excusing the prick as he went out, farther into the property, and beyond the fence line, too, chopping down trees. He'd had no bloody clue what it meant to be a farmer. Chopped and culled but hardly grew more'n a vegetable patch on the parcel of scrub he took up after the war. Not enough land to make a go of it, but it'd eased the stinking government's conscience, probably, to give something to the motley bunch that made it back.

David sits without speaking. He's waiting on him to finish his story, no doubt.

'I held back enlisting so long,' Len finally says, 'because I had to run the miserable excuse of a farm for Ma. She had nobody else. Held on until there was no bloody choice but to go – call me a coward, but I'm not ashamed of that fact.'

He always dresses the story up for Davo. Skips over the darkest bits. Tells how Mary, Joe's missus, used to call in while they were out on the verandah recuperatin', making out she was doin' her rounds, telling 'em to behave 'emselves, and not show her up. Evie'd be regularly popping by with little treats she'd baked, too, sneaking Olive in to see her old man and Uncle Joe. Sometimes, if she was looking after Hazel and her brother Harry while Mary worked, Evie'd bring all the littlies in and they'd sit there, quietly playing on the edge of the verandah, until three became a crowd and one of them started squawking or crying.

'Like a bloody summer holiday by the sea. If yer stretched the imagination hard.'

Len likes his chats with Joe's younger brother, though Davo doesn't say much. More contained than his brother, serious like, doesn't take the time to play around like Joe. He's a good *mother*, though. Keeps the mug of tea topped up, and occasionally waves the plate containing a couple a slabs of his mother's fruitcake in Len's general direction.

Feels a bit sorry for Davo, Len does. There were ten years between him and Joe. Lived in his brother's shadow. And Joe was a bit of a local hero. Done it all, he had. Got married and had a family, took his place running the family property, fought a war for his country. Died of his injuries, a slow and protracted death – four years of war followed by three years of dying. Eternally brave, that man.

'There's not much,' Len says, a little less wobbly now that the beers have been sopped up with the Bushells tea, 'not much that me and your brother didn't talk about.'

'That's good to hear, Len. He thought you were a good bloke, too.'

Len doesn't know what to say to that. He's a bit choked up, if the truth be known. He's wishing now that Mrs Smith'd turn up. Come home early from the CWA bake-off, or church meeting, or whatever it is she gets up to on a Wednesday arvo.

David surprises him then, tells him that since Joe's passing his ma's been keeping herself busy, trying to forget, probably, that in the past two years she's lost both a husband and a son. His voice tapers off to barely a whisper. 'The pride-and-joy son, at that.'

Len tries to find the right words to say. He expects that Davo is just as much a pride and joy to his mother as Joe was, but what would he know? He's relieved when he changes the subject.

'How is Evelyn, and little Olive?'

Len starts at that. Nobody's called Evie that for as long as he can recollect. That was how he'd been introduced to her. *Miss Evelyn Henderson*. In town for three weeks before the start of the war, she was, to help out old Doc Allan just before he was due to retire. Never woulda thought he'd go to the quack to have a chat about the knotted-up feeling in his guts – probably just indigestion that wouldn't go away, according to the doc – and come out with an arrangement to have afternoon tea with the prettiest girl he'd ever laid his eyes on.

He notes how long his quiet has lasted and shakes himself back into the present.

'Sorry, mate. Heat's taking it outta me. I was just thinking. Life, eh? Yeah, she's good. Tired, with the baby coming soon. But she'll be right. Tough girl, my Evie. And Olive's still as cheeky as a whip.'

Len yawns big and covers his mouth.

'Bit weary meself these days.'

He doesn't sleep much since he came back. It was starting to improve after the first year or so went by. Things were starting to feel more settled inside. But with Joe passing unexplained like that when he was supposed to have been getting better, the night terrors have returned. Many's the night Evie's come out to the kitchen to find him sitting by the fire with it stacked up and blazing away. She'd go over and fling open the sash windows, saying she needed to let some fresh air into the hotbox, and he'd make out like he'd been caught sleeping. He'd be shivering, though. Wrapped up in a dirty great blanket but still he couldn't get warm. Chilled beyond the bone. Ground into his core, that cold. Tried to hide it. Didn't want Evie to know that he was worrying that he might be losing his marbles again. Bad enough he's down a foot without going cuckoo on her, too. Only one who understood any of that, only one he ever spoke to out loud about it, was Joe, the bloody bastard.

He chuckles, remembering how after they came home they could really knock 'em back. Even though Joe was supposed to be recuperating and off the grog, he'd sneak 'em in and Mary'd turn a blind eye. Some nights they'd keep talking until the sun came up. Joe'd had his own demons, of course. Some nights they didn't talk about any of it at all. Just sat in silence, and that helped, a bit. Going inside himself and not feeling he had to explain his thoughts and actions to a worried wife was somehow curative. That, and being able to poke fun and laugh at the dirtiest, grimiest bastard stuff of life with a couple or more medicinal rums under the belt.

Len picks up the half-empty mug. Clasps it in both hands. Breathes deeply into his mug, inhaling the pungent black Bushells scent.

'Missed this brew,' he says, turning to the open back door. The breeze seems to have picked up the tiniest bit. 'Not likely to be a break in the weather anytime soon.'

Finally, he gets around to what he came to say all along.

'Decided to sell up the back half, Davo. Hardly enough land left to call meself a farmer.'

Everyone tells him he's doing real well. But he knows his limitations. He's smart enough to figure that he'll continue to get better and faster with time. But it's more than just his foot that they took from him. Might take years for him to work at full pace. He tires easily, mind goes off on tangents. He forgets things, too. Started thinking again about the months leading up to that bloody hospital ship a while back. Hasn't been quite right since. Recalled lying there on that hospital bed on the way back to Fremantle, fully knowing he'd be as useless as tits on a bull to Evie. Practically willed a torpedo to come out of somewhere and sink them all. At least there'd be hope of a pension for her then. It was bloody Joe what took those thoughts away, made him laugh again.

He'd ended up lying facedown out on the damp grass by the chook house that night when the thoughts came back to dog him. Evie'd found him. Worried sick, she was, to wake and find the door wide open and him gone. He didn't have a bloody clue why he was out there, or even remember going out. Left his cane inside. Must've hobbled out in his sleep, forgot he couldn't walk without it, or something. Tried to hide his wet face from Evie as she held him close and forced him to love her. He couldn't feel a thing, but she persisted anyway. Said to her, when she climbed off him, that he thought there'd been a fox out there, working the chooks into a frenzy. She'd cried then, and gone back inside. He'd stayed there a bit longer, forcing himself up and inside before the sun fully rose and little Olive came out and started ramming questions down his throat.

He takes a swig of tea. Avoids Davo's eye as he finishes what he'd come to say.

'Smiths can have first option, if youse want it.'

When he'd raised the notion of selling the back blocks, Evie'd seemed relieved, joyful, even. He had an inkling that she'd misunderstood for a moment or two. Thought he meant to sell up altogether. Leave the farm. He knows she thinks she wasn't really cut out for this life. City girl at heart, though to her credit she'd given life here a bloody good go. Took at least ten years of dancing classes before the war. Liked to go to plays and acted in the local repertory company. Imagined she was headed for something bigger and better than falling for him, no doubt.

When he saw that split second of joy flash through her, he'd felt betrayed all over again. She *wanted* to leave. He could've said they'd sell up in that moment, let her parents help find a job for him in a shop or an office or something befitting half a man with a hobble. But just the thought of that had made him shudder. She'd just told him about expecting another baby, too, and he didn't want no kid of his growing up to be citified.

He told her it would be good for them to sell up some of the land. They could make the house bigger with the money. Get a few luxuries to make life a bit easier for them both. Take Olive for a proper holiday, to Sydney maybe, and see that Luna Park he'd heard all about. He hardly ever went near the back half of the property, anyway. His old man'd never got around to clearing or fencing it properly before he took his last walk out there and carked it in the scrub. He'd never had the interest to try and make a go of it himself. After his mum passed, he didn't feel he needed to make use of the land. Didn't feel he had to prove anything to anyone anymore.

There're things he can't talk about with anybody at all, now that Joe's passed. He came here today feeling lonesome and half thinking that maybe something of Joe would be there in his little brother. Thought that he could perhaps raise some of the stuff he's been keeping bottled up. Maybe he could keep it light to start. Try telling Davo that he's wondered on occasion if they've held a community meeting to come up with ways to try and keep him chirpy. It's odd, he'll say, how they lean into him when they speak and pat him on the arm. Smile at him bigger than usual, like he's some sort of special case. They'll pull him up in the main street, or at church when Evie whinges hard enough so that he makes a token appearance. Some of the oldies talk at him slowly and loudly, too, enunciate their sounds carefully so you'd think it was his brain that was removed, not his foot. It's almost laughable, the way that Louis Fraser's kid stamps his bankbook each week and pauses, like he's got something profound to say, then hands the book over, all respectful like, with the biggest, dopiest grin Len reckons he's ever seen.

But old Mrs Smith comes in then, fussing and bustling about, and pulls him in and holds him so close and tight when he stands up that he's embarrassed by his own neediness. It was Joe who was the war hero, not him. And Joe's gone. He's just the dumb bastard who got stretchered out of Changi at the end, with a septic foot and troppo brain. Nothing heroic about that. Stayed alive for the duration, that's about all he'd managed. *Alive for the duration*. That'd make a good epitaph. But he's not going to say anything about any of that. Not here in this house of sadness. He's lucky, he's alive, and he should be grateful that all these people care enough about him to be nice, even when he slips up and gets sloshed in the middle of the week. No point in disturbing good folks just going about their daily business of getting on with life. Not their problem, where he's been and what he's seen. Diggers in the First saw worse'n them, anyway, by some accounts.

He excuses himself. Tells 'em he'll go home and get on with doing what needs to be done to make amends with Evie for skiving off in the middle of the day. Give them some time to think about whether they want the land. He'll keep the rest to himself. Nobody wants to hear what goes on inside his head, or his miserable concerns, either. He'd only ever confided in Joe about the big one – seeing his missus sneaking out in her pretty green city dress while he was laid up and feeling sorry for his lot. A spring in her step, she had.

She's having a baby, that's the good thing to come of all this. Olive's not going to be a lonely kid like he was. She'll have a brother or sister. Doesn't matter how the baby came to be, or that he can't make the sums add up. He'll love it all the same. Just because he doesn't remember even being up to the job of making a nipper doesn't mean he wasn't. His head's messed up. He forgets stuff. No secrets there. She lay down in the grass that morning he was out there and said she loved him more than life and tried to show him how much. That's when they made the baby, she says. Then this morning, before he came into town, he was thinking about that pretty green dress and where she might've last worn it, and how her belly'd grown out awful quick. She said it again. Pulled him close and said she'd be patient, and that they'd be right. It reminded him a bit of that night he proposed. He couldn't quite believe she actually said yes.

That she'd be willing to give up city living for life in the scrub with the likes of him. But he accepted that she had, ready enough, and was so happy that he'd cried right there on his knees in front of her. Soft bastard.

Olive came out of her room then, made him be a monster, chase her with his clunking wooden foot. Squealing and laughing as she let him catch her. He shook his foot off and made out like he'd wipe his ugly scarred stump all over her belly. She jumped up and ran outside. Then came back and planted a kiss on his cheek. He'd felt pretty damn good to be alive in that moment. Maybe that was enough to be getting on with.

1956

Unchained

'Al Hibbler. I had it sent from America.' He sounds impressed with himself.

Taking her arm, he guides her to the club chair next to the record player and says to wait. Tells her he will be back soon. He's that close she can feel his breath on her face when he speaks. She pulls back, hoping that he doesn't notice her hand is shaking. She's about to ask where his old pride and joy, the gramophone, has gone. But by then he's gone, too.

She sits, smoothing the flared skirt of her dress over her knees, and looks around, taking in all the detail. She recognises the photograph in the corner of him in his graduation robes, his parents proudly and stiffly posed beside him. The bureau it sits on is new, as is the record player and the painting over the fireplace: an Aboriginal man leaning on a spear and standing on one leg. She notes the feminine touches – a bunch of yellow roses in a blue vase, a rug in front of the fire, colourful crocheted cushions on all the chairs. It is not the room she'd have expected for a still-single professional man.

She envies Flora Sinclair, for her role as his housekeeper and cook. Imagines they must have scintillating conversations when he slips out here from his consulting rooms at lunch and afternoon tea time. She misses adult conversation.

No, she misses *their* conversations.

Noticing the scarlet tassel hanging from his old gramophone on the other side of the room, she envies her again – Flora ruddy Sinclair – for her privileged position of working for the doctor, for having free rein in his home. Envies her, too, for her uncomplicated widow status, one that will not attract unwanted attention from the town gossips. Feels bad now for allowing such thoughts to enter her mind.

She wishes she could speak of the ache that sits behind the shield she wraps around her marriage. To do so would be disloyal – as disloyal, at least, as being here. She imagines the ache as a tool, an ugly, rusted cast-iron gadget that grinds deeper with each traitorous thought. Although it is the truth, she doesn't dare say out loud that she is tired of being responsible for maintaining the facade of a normal family life. That she's sick of nursing and nurturing; of being incapable of fully engaging with her own pain, or joy. Who would she say it to, anyway, without it making things awkward, and causing more trouble?

He's clinking something in the kitchen, preparing a pot of tea. In the past, the ritual of tea preparation enabled her to feel less disloyal in the lead-up to their interactions. Together, they'd drink tea, prepared in the pot his mother had bought for him. He'd told her that she'd given it to him in the hope it would help him impress a good woman. She'd thought that hilarious. She'd been impressed enough, she'd said, by the intricate detail of the pot, though she was clearly not a good woman.

A few minutes pass before he returns with a tray. Two glasses. A smaller one, sherry, for her. Something heavier, an inch of golden treacle in the bottom of a thick crystal glass, for him. She is surprised. She never drinks alcohol. He'd have remembered that before. She cannot abide the stuff, has not touched a drop since Len's first leave. He'd come home to her angry and drunk. But apologetic and distraught when she'd told him how much he'd upset her. Not so apologetic when he returned home for good, though. Angry and drunk had since become his default setting.

He sits on the chair opposite hers, a low, highly polished table between them, and leans in to clink her glass. Not noticing, or choosing not to notice, that she does not drink his offering. He thanks her for coming – as though it was his idea.

'I knew you'd come, Evie.'

She bristles at the tone of his voice. She's irritated by his arrogance, his presumption of knowing her mind, and by the lack of tea. But she shapes the corners of her mouth into what she hopes bears some semblance of a smile. She wants him to see that she does not bear grudges, that she has grown and has moved beyond what was – or was not, as it turned out. They sit, not speaking, for a few moments before he clears his throat and gets up and moves towards the record player.

'I'm not here for music, Stan. I have an appointment.' His name sounds odd, leaving her mouth. For several years she has forced herself, even mentally, to refer to him as *Doctor Wilson*. It was the only way. Her voice wobbles and betrays her. Even *Stanley* would have been a better choice.

He looks at her and she feels the blood rush to her cheeks. She's transparent. Five pm is an odd time to request an appointment. Everybody around here knows that he prefers to stop seeing patients at three-thirty. And that Flora Sinclair goes home at four to her children.

'Listen. And then, if you wish, we'll go back out there and I will take your temperature and pulse.' He tilts his head towards the door leading back to the consulting room and lifts the arm of the record player, placing the needle down carefully.

She remembers saying once that the crackling sound before the music began made the hairs on the back of her neck stand on end. That the anticipation confused her senses similarly to the way that a fast drop in barometric pressure immediately preceding a storm shook her into alertness. Until recently she'd thought she could recall each and every conversation they'd had as her need to reflect on them arose. But she no longer remembers his response to what she'd said on that day.

As the crackling is subsumed by the instrumental introduction, he looks into her eyes and holds her gaze. She swallows and looks away at the painting on the wall. The music, with its explicit lyrics of longing and regret, is too obvious. She recalls that awful night when it all became too much. Len taunting her – calling her a *jezebel*, a *harlot*. Telling her to go to him. Not to come back and expect him to raise her bastard.

Her body tenses. The music was never like this before. It was subtle, evocative. German baroque, Beethoven's *Moonlight Sonata*. No words necessary. Ample room for the imagination to fill the abundance of space. Seductive music, to alert the senses. These lyrics, with their *hunger* and *need*, crowd her.

She puts her untouched drink down on the polished table. Remains composed. Holds his gaze. He smiles. The set-up is contrived. The atmosphere, the dimmed lamps and drawn curtains, sordid. Worst of all, she is too obvious in her good green dress and splash of pink lipstick, saved all these years for special occasions. *Jezebel. Harlot.* She should not have come here like this, ever again. But especially not while poor Len lies there, drying out, in that hospital bed. She recalls her mother's voice as she'd said goodbye after marrying Len and setting out to catch the train to her new home in the country. *You make a choice. Then you live with it.* Strange and unexpected words even for her to have uttered.

She looks at the painting. Recalls the pushy door-to-door salesman traipsing out to all the farms a few years earlier, attempting to force oil paintings of noble warriors and submissive women onto those with little money to spare after the war. And the story he'd spun of being an artist, *great fan of the Heidelberg set*, he'd said. And, remembering the paintings lining the walls of the home of the parents of the dental student from Nedlands she'd once thought she loved, told him to go on and share his story.

He'd spoken of having the desire to see the country outside Melbourne, of coming across to the west and heading as far north as you could go. Stuck there during the wet season, he'd gone into the desert and asked blackfellas and lubras if he could pay them to allow him to paint them. She'd never heard the word *lubra* used before. It hadn't sounded like the right word to use for a woman. Still, she'd been taken by one of the paintings of a woman with a child hiding behind her legs, just his face showing. And her defiant expression, challenging the viewer by looking straight ahead – confronting head-on – not dropping her eyes demurely like the rest of the painted women. She'd felt a stab of pain in her chest, seeing the boy, and the mother – it had to be the mother – protecting him from potential danger. She'd felt herself disappearing then, and grabbed at the wooden hatstand inside the door to try and stop herself falling. Once she composed herself, she'd reassured the worried salesman that she was okay. She'd desperately wanted that painting then, to remind her never to forget, to punish herself further for not protecting her own boy. She wanted to invite the salesman in, to tell him everything. She'd failed her boy, had been unable to prevent him wandering off into the bush. In those few muddled moments, she'd imagined the woman painting her own grief, subtly subversive, slapping the paint on the canvas and demanding her share of the payment for a loss that could never be recompensed.

She'd been about to ask *How much?* Then she turned the painting over and saw it had been stamped in tiny letters *Taiwan*. She'd handed it back and closed the door on the salesman's face, more isolated than she'd been just a few seconds earlier.

'It's fake,' she says, pointing to the painting, 'painted in Taiwan. Why would you want that on your wall?'

He smiles at her, says nothing. Cups his hand to his ear, indicating, as he used to, *listen to the music*. It comes across as condescending and angers her.

'I need to pick up Olive soon.'

She looks down and scratches at a non-existent mark on her dress. She hopes that Olive is not too upset by having been dropped at her friend Hazel's house to sleep the night, without explanation – or with an explanation that was clearly a lie. *Going to talk to the doctor about your father's treatment. I'll finish late. You can stay overnight. You'll have fun.* Her voice had been too bright to be believable. The look Olive gave her assured her of that.

She wonders if he remembers the last time she'd worn the dress here. It had been tight on the waist then, her secret already threatening to reveal itself. Of the way they'd joked beforehand about stitching a big scarlet *A* onto the mint coloured chest, so everyone knew what a brazen woman she was. And afterwards, her secret shared, of the way that, despite her tears and protestations, he'd sent her home to a life of respectability with her daughter and her broken-down husband, *the only one* who could be the father of her unborn child.

In those first months after he came home, whenever the new doctor had knocked on the door Len hobbled out of sight, up to the back shed. Or he'd lock himself in the bedroom and refuse to come out or speak. Initially, she'd been embarrassed. After a while, grateful to have someone to talk to – someone who wasn't always angry, or drunk more often than sober. Sometimes they'd wind up in the kitchen, seated at the laminex-topped table under the window, sharing a pot of tea. And if Olive was napping, while he devoured a plateful of her freshly and specially made biscuits, they'd talk, firstly of Len and of little Olive, and later of other matters. She'd wondered early on, but refrained from ever actually asking, what would make a relatively young doctor come all the way from Sydney to a small town in Western Australia. Why here? Why hadn't he enlisted? How had *he* avoided being damaged in Singapore, New Guinea or Europe, as so many of the district's men had?

She tried not to grizzle to him too much. She'd made her choice, now she lived with it. She'd got off lightly, *she* hadn't had to go to fight. She counted down the days until his visits, but once he was there she'd wished that she could talk to him about the fact that she was almost consumed with trying to make her husband strong, struggling to raise a toddler, and keeping the bank from marching in and demanding a fat cheque. Barnaby Lister was a decent man, but there was only so far she could push the returned soldier line when every family with a man over twenty-two or twenty-three was likely to be in the same boat. She was humiliated by the fact that other people seemed to be resuming normal lives, putting the past behind them and moving on. She couldn't imagine anyone else in the district crawling into Barney Lister's office and pleading for more time to come up with loan repayments.

She didn't pick up on his signals initially, but thought retrospectively that the shift must have happened that day he'd confessed to feeling lonely, missing life in the city, and lamenting the lack of live music in a small country town. *Call me Stan*, he'd said that day. *'Doctor' is too formal for us.* The energy in the air between them was palpable. She justified to herself what was happening. Len deserved this. He'd pushed her towards Stan, so he'd have to live with it. She showed Stan the family gramophone player and records her mother had given her to bring out to this *godforsaken place* after she'd married Len, *just six months after meeting him*, and they'd laughed at her impersonation of a disapproving mother. She could have told him, then, of the first loss she'd experienced, of the disintegration of all the dreams she'd carried in adolescence of a future filled with art, music and dance. That when her student dentist was killed, it had been the possibility of an enhanced life she had missed, more than the student dentist himself.

But instead they'd spoken of classical music, and of the amateur repertory theatre she'd performed in before marrying Len and moving away from the city to live here. He'd boasted of his own collection of music at home – four rooms at the back of the consulting rooms – and said that one day she should come and listen. It had all seemed perfectly acceptable.

And although now it feels anything but acceptable to be in this position, here she is again.

Before calling to make an appointment with him earlier in the day, she'd struggled with her conscience. In the months after Petey died, Olive had been withdrawn, particularly with Len. Over time, she'd improved, but had never returned to being the gregarious child she'd been before the accident. Lately, her behaviour has regressed. She hasn't been so remote since those first months after losing her brother. At the same time, despite wanting to discuss her concerns about Olive, Evelyn had felt a consuming need to be in his company. Of course it wouldn't do, after nearly nine years, to turn up and say that she was intolerably lonely and for now – but not forever – needed to spend a little time with him, just a few hours.

She'd decided she'd ask if maybe he could speak to Olive. Olive might confide in him, his being a doctor and all. She'd say then that she was wondering if perhaps children were not always as resilient as people assumed. She'd confess her fears that both she and Len had let Olive down – Len by resuming his heavy drinking, and she, angry, by shutting down her heart, being unable to push aside the burden of her own grief to give enough of herself to her daughter. She'd been wondering, she'd ask, if he had some medical books she could read, for she'd been thinking lately that maybe not talking about what happened in life could be more damaging to everybody concerned than being open about it.

But now she's here, in her too-obvious dress and lips, and the matter of transparency cannot be ignored. She won't speak of Olive, of Len. Those concerns must sit close to her, inside her shield.

She's been pathetic, holding on to that thread of hope. She sees that now. She knew, even before she revealed her secret that day, that things had already begun to change. She'd sensed, sitting there beside him the past few times, listening to his music, that he'd become distracted, less open with her. He'd been short, judgemental of her request for him to play particular music that made her feel good inside. *Vivaldi is lowbrow*, he'd said. *I thought your tastes were maturing*. She'd laughed and challenged him to tell her why he felt that she needed to mature, but he'd refused to respond. She was being foolish. And she was laughing too much, he'd said, as he led her to his bedroom at the back of the house without even pretence at being unable to resist her. *What is* wrong *with you?* She realised he'd grown bored with his small-town dalliance, while she'd pretended until that moment that nothing was wrong at all. In their time together, she'd managed to forget the rest of it. She was grateful to spend this time, whether half an hour, or several hours, in his company before going home to try and repair her husband.

It had never felt this way in the past. Then, the chemistry, or whatever it was that made two people feel breathless in the company of the other, overruled all else. Now, that has gone and has been replaced by him, too contrived. And her, too obvious. He'd told her in what was to be the last time they were together in his bed that he couldn't be the father of her unborn child, that *the only one who could be the father to her unborn child was Len*. She cried, but said she understood what he meant. She would not try to force him into a corner. He had his reputation, and couldn't be throwing that away on the likes of her. She'd just wanted him to acknowledge the possibility. She told him that her own father, so she'd discovered on the day she'd married Len, was not her real father, but he'd been the only one she'd known. *Different circumstances, of course. My father died. In the first war, and his best friend stepped up to the challenge of...us.*

That wasn't what he'd meant, he said, dismissing her and showing no interest in the story that still upset her, even to think about. He said it was impossible for him to sire a child. *Impossible*, and he'd pointed to his now-flaccid penis as though that was evidence enough to prove his sterility. He went on, then, to say that he had in fact lost a marriage because of this failure of nature to follow its expected course. It was the first time he'd mentioned that he, too, was married.

She'd never really believed him, and perhaps Len hadn't believed her story, either. But from the moment she came home from Stan's bed that day – reminding Len in a quavering voice of that cold pre-dawn morning when she'd gone to him while he was outside in the garden, how they'd made love for the first time since his return from the war – he'd never called her those despicable names again. It was decided that she'd go to the next town to have the baby – a bigger hospital and better facilities, she'd told Len, who'd nodded and agreed it would be better. And once little Petey was born, while she watched him closely, trying to spot hints to determine the truth, Len adored and accepted him as the gentle family member he'd been for his brief time with them.

She stands as the song finishes, recalling as she does so that trip to the coast with Len and Olive the summer after Petey died, both of them determined to make a fresh start. They'd left Olive with the kindly lady who'd run the boarding house so they could go and see *Casablanca*, the movie they'd seen together the night after Len first struck up the courage to talk to her. She'd adored that film, and taken as a positive sign the fact that it was playing in the town hall of the little coastal town they were visiting. The film had formed a part of the fabric of their shared life. *Play it, Sam, play 'As Time Goes By.'* She'd sworn that was what Ingrid Bergman's character had said. But Len'd misheard – according to her – for he believed Bogart had said: *Play it again, Sam.*

In their first years together, she'd recount her version of the lines to Len when she wanted to relax for a few minutes and listen to music. And he'd say his to her when a song he enjoyed finished and he'd wanted to hear it again. Sitting through the movie on that trip to the coast, she'd felt herself tensing as the moment those words were to be uttered approached. After all they'd already been through as a couple and family, it mattered to her that this time, although she already knew it couldn't be so, Len be right. Perhaps then, she told herself, they could laugh about it and build a new happy memory to draw on when looking back on this fresh-start phase of their lives.

Bergman had said her line and his jaw had set, just a fraction. He'd reached for her hand, glanced across at her and, shrugging, had whispered, *Right as always, my dear.* And she'd smiled and felt hopeful that one day they'd find a way to crawl through the web of grief, and possibly even escape it, together.

'Don't play it again.' She leans towards Stan and, taking his right hand loosely in hers, shakes it. 'I'm going to visit Len.'

1960

The lie Paul Carmody told Hazel

Friday afternoon, second last period.

'Don't forget, *colour*, in our country, is spelt with a *U*. We do not – I repeat, *do not* – live in America. Use your *Us*.'

Olive is busting for the end of this year. Then, she'll finally get to discard her ugly military green school uniform. Her father's precious new car is a minty shade of green. Her mother has a full-skirted pretty green dress packed in a camphor chest in her bedroom. She never wears it anymore, at least as far as Olive can recall. She'd like a mint green dress, too, when she's done with school. She'll wear it every chance she gets. *She* won't hide it away, taking it out to dance about with it held against her body when she thinks nobody is home to see her.

'In parts of Asia and the Middle East, green is the colour of Islam. In Ireland green is of cultural and religious significance, too.'

Olive looks up and snickers as Yvonne Wilkins interrupts Miss Jones. 'Are leprechauns Catholic or Protestant?'

Green for go.

'Leave this room, Yvonne Wilkins! Now!' Miss Jones turns pink from her neck to her nose.

Olive leans over and whispers to Hazel that when she gets her driver's licence she will take the mint green car and her mother's pretty green dress and go far away from the farm and find excitement.

Olive grins as Hazel's eyes widen in astonishment. Everyone in the district knows that her father's new FB utility, bought on hire-purchase, is his pride and joy. He'd throttle her if she took it so far as the farm gate.

They've both got Plain Jane names befitting females of their mothers' generation. Olive suspects that the two women, longtime friends and pregnant together, conspired to ensure that if girls popped out of their bodies, they were to be allocated bland names as a means of ensuring they stayed tethered to the precious land, as *they* were. There's no way that will happen, though. She's got plans and they don't involve either wheat or sheep, or being a farm-wife. Hazel, though, she's a good girl. She'll do her name justice. She'll get married and raise a brood of sensibly named children. Perhaps she'll become a country nursing sister first, like her mother, and bring another generation of country bumpkins into the world. If Hazel had a colour, it would be beige. Beige for old-lady and nice-girl sensible undergarments.

'Eyes to the front, please, Olive...Red in Communist China signifies joy or luck and is used in some Eastern cultures for weddings and funerals.'

In red pencil, Olive doodles a broken-in-two heart in the margin and scrawls *James Dean* in one side and her own movie star name in the other. Miss Jones holds up a photograph to prove that she has travelled and had a life before becoming an *educator, not a teacher* in this claustrophobic little town. It is the second time this term that she's found an excuse to show the photo. Travelling with her parents to convert the heathens is possibly the only adventure that Miss Jones has experienced in her life. While the other girls in the class seem to find the photo inspiring and ask questions of Miss Jones about her experiences, Olive finds it disturbing. Mysterious women, in vibrant red silks, bells and beads and with hennaed hands, stare compliantly at the lens. Beside them, a younger Miss Jones, lumpy and gawky, poses with a forced smile in her buttoned-to-the-throat shirt and ankle-length skirt. Virginal Miss Jones, who'd spent her late teens in exotic locations with her parents, helping those less fortunate, now waits for a farmer to ride up on his white stallion and whisk her away to a life of perpetual nappy washing and weather forecast monitoring. Virginal white for schoolteachers, innocent babies and the lie of Western church weddings.

It's her father's annual get-together with his mates up in the city. A day and night reminiscing about the days he vehemently refuses to speak of for the other 364 days of the year. He'll be home tomorrow night, or the next day if he's really bunged one on and can't point the car in the right direction. One year he lost his false foot. Hilarious, he thought it was, as he told Olive and her mother about setting up a search party to find it.

She's supposed to go straight home after school to help her mother, who'll pretend to worry when she doesn't get off the bus but really won't mind too much. It's the one day and night off from making his meat and three veg – one white, one orange, one green – that her mother gets each year.

Behind the shelter sheds, Olive lines her eyelids in heavy black kohl before crossing the road and walking straight past the bus. Black for one year of European women's mourning. When Mr Giovanni died several years earlier, Mrs Giovanni began wearing drab black garments and headscarves about town. After that, for a while when she was alone in her room Olive took to draping herself in a black cloth she'd found folded in the back of the linen cupboard and crossing her chest dramatically while weeping crocodile tears in front of the mirror. Sometimes she'd really cry, but not for Mr Giovanni.

She waves to Hazel to get off the bus and accompany her on today's probable non-adventure, but Hazel shrugs and shakes her head. No doubt she's thinking that it's Guides night, and she can't miss that.

Olive is aware that since that day last year when Hazel arrived at the farm at the wrong time, and sneaked away, thinking that neither Olive nor her father had seen her, her friend has been on a futile mission to keep Olive on the straight and narrow. She imagines telling Hazel that she mostly doesn't feel the pain of her father's disciplinary measures, but she no longer knows what is appropriate to discuss when it comes to the private business of her own family, or other people's.

She strides down the street, blackened eyes matching her increasingly darkening mood. There's no escaping her own mind, and there's nowhere to go and nothing to do other than watch the under-eighteens train for tomorrow's Anzac Day game. What a dump town. She sometimes thinks that living in town would be almost worse than being stuck on the farm. At least there she can disappear from view for hours at a time if she wishes. She looks up and pokes her tongue out as Hazel gives her one last anxious gaze and half-wave from the back window of the bus. Tomorrow, after she has done her weekly chores, she expects that Hazel will visit her, and try again to get her to join the Guides. She'd have succeeded last time if only she could have made Olive see beyond the pledges of duty and honour to God and the Queen.

Turning left, Olive passes the cemetery and the old soldiers' home and heads towards the station. She'll stop there and have one of the cigarettes she nicked out of her father's packet before she gets changed and goes to the oval.

Now that the new highway is complete and they've reduced the number of trains coming through the district, the station is little more than a barely-used siding. But as is always the case in this town, the old ways prevail and they'll keep calling it a station for the next hundred years. Not that it matters. Maybe in a hundred years a bomb will have been dropped on the town, and there won't be a railway or a district to quibble about.

Things rarely change around these parts; babies are born to grow up and marry others from the district. They make more babies to replace both those that don't grow up, and those that have grown old and been shunted off to the old fogeys' home to await death. Her father's and grandfather's wars hadn't changed the balance all that much. Some people had just ended up in different cemeteries in parts of the world they'd never have imagined they'd visit. After her dad's war, other people came to town, some from those same countries that her father's friends remained in – six feet under the ground – so it all balanced out in an odd way.

Her mother had made her think about that just this morning while her father was outside, double and triple checking that his precious car was ready for the drive up to the city. Her mother had turned to her, a wan little strip of a smile almost visible on her lips, and said, *New car, same old tired routine.* Realising, then, the never-ending sameness of their lives, Olive felt as though she'd bonded a little with her mother. And that maybe, at last, her mother had forgiven her. She decided then that this weekend, while her father was out drinking and living the high life with his old army buddies, she was going to celebrate the maybe-forgiveness and do something reckless and unexpected.

As the wrought-iron bench and weathered station come into view, she slows down and pulls her ponytail free from the rubber bands, wincing as a clump of hair catches. She moves towards the bench and, pulling her schoolbag off her shoulder, dumps it on the seat. Unclipping the buckle, she reaches in to check that her dress and shoes haven't disappeared throughout the school day. She's about to pull them out and go around the back to get changed when Paul Carmody calls out to her from across the tracks.

Since winning the 'Best and Fairest' in the under-eighteens last year, when Paul Carmody walks he puffs his chest up and his arms swing like an orangutan's. She grimaces as she remembers that Hazel had told her recently that she'd let him touch her at the movies. Though Olive had laughed and asked for all the details, she had been sickened at the mental image of one hulking ape-like hand covering both of Hazel's substantially proportioned breasts in the back row of the Saturday matinee.

Grabbing at his revolting crotch, he asks her for a kiss, accompanying the request with gyrations, dirty laughter and lip-smacking sounds. She yells out and asks him if he is aware that his maroon blazer from St Ignatius's school is the same colour as that worn by some Buddhist monks.

'What would your Pope think about that?'

For a moment she thinks about crossing the tracks – just to shock him. His pimply face would probably explode if she strode across, grabbed his yellow and brown stripey tie and pulled him close to kiss him on the lips. If it weren't for the fact that Hazel thinks that she is in love with repulsive Paul Carmody, Olive may have followed through. That would be reckless and unexpected enough for one day. He grabs again at his crotch and wriggles his hips about, so that she's reminded of a rutting ram at the back end of a ewe in the paddock.

That's when she sees him. She decides there and then that when she tells Hazel about the afternoon, she'll claim that Roberto still looks like James Dean, all lean and arrogant. Though this is not strictly true, he does have a more lustrous head of hair than she's seen on anyone other than perhaps the real, forever young, James Dean, whose photograph she keeps tucked in the pages of an old *Girls' Own Annual* in the secret space between her mattress and the sprung bed base.

He must've been there all along, leaning against the far side of the old railway's office, as though he'd known she was coming. He's got a tatty book in his hand, but he's lowered it and is watching them, a smirk on his face. She's not afraid. Rather, she's emboldened as she turns back to Paul Carmody and tells him to run along like a good boy to footy training and when he gets there to ask one of his bum buddies to grab his thing for him and give it a good tug.

She notices that Paul Carmody has spotted Roberto leaning against the weatherboard siding wall. He looks embarrassed, and she's about to yell and ask if he's sorry about being caught propositioning her or he's just shamed at being caught grabbing his own little pecker. But he turns and, calling her a tart, hoists his schoolbag over his shoulder and takes off at a pace somewhere between a fast walk and a slow run.

Now she's alone with him. It is not only reckless and unexpected that she be here, but stupid and risky, too. Being alone with a member of the male species – any male, but most particularly this male – is at the top of the ever-expanding list of inappropriate behaviours devised by her increasingly illogical father. If he were to appear now in his mint green car, he'd demand that she get in, drive her home, and, without asking a single question, beat her until she could no longer walk, just as he had that day when she'd told her mother and Mrs Giovanni what had really gone on in the back rooms of Giovannis' Emporium.

'I thought Buddhists wore orange robes.'

His voice is deeper than she remembers. She sits down on the bench seat and, reaching inside her schoolbag for one of her father's cigarettes, tries not to tremble.

'Most do,' she says, 'but these ones are from a particular order. My virginal missionary teacher knows all about these things.'

'The Order of Maroon?' He moves closer, stops about six feet away from her, sits on his khaki duffel bag and raises his arms. Khaki – for murder and mayhem, Anzac Day drunken tirades, and wasted lives.

'I come in peace.'

'Yes,' she says, scrabbling in the bottom of her schoolbag for the box of matches she'd stashed under her pencil tin. She's been building her armour tighter around her since that day. She's glad she's piled it all on today – the bravado of her tough-girl routine, the harsh black lines around her eyes, the cigarettes. 'The Order of Maroon consists mostly of frustrated and repressed teenage boys. Richer than us public school students, they will grow up to run this miserable excuse for a town, with their beige wives loyally at their sides, grateful…always grateful and obedient.'

James Dean laughs. 'Nothing beige about you, Miss Olive Grove.'

She'd forgotten that he'd once called her that, and she's shaking a bit as she strikes the match and raises it to the cigarette between her lips. 'Don't call me that. I'm changing my name as soon as I can. Everyone'll call me Natalie, then.'

She stands and moves closer to him, and asks if he knew that she'd told them the truth – his mother, her mother and father, everybody who would listen to her story – but they hadn't believed her.

He reaches for the cigarette, and a tingle jolts through her fingertips as their hands touch.

'They didn't want to believe it,' he says. 'They'd never have believed it. So I had to leave, fast, and save any more drama.'

'And now you're back.'

That same year Mr Giovanni died, before she'd ever called Roberto James Dean, Olive had decided that being a goody-two-shoes wasn't making life at home any easier for her father, or for her. So far, her rebellions had been relatively small. A missed class here and there, the odd broken curfew and sneaking into the movies without paying for a ticket.

She had spoken to Roberto as he served behind the counter of his parents' shop at least once a month for much of her life. But he'd been away at university in the city all year and seemed different. She'd just seen *Rebel Without a Cause* again at the pictures, sneaking in to the matinee after it started so nobody would report to her parents that she'd been there. She'd tried to make a joke when she saw him, said that, sitting on the back steps of Giovannis' Emporium, he looked a bit like James Dean, with all that hair and the cigarette hanging out of the corner of his mouth. He didn't respond, and didn't even seem to care that a girl had caught him crying. Not at first. She'd sat down, self-conscious about the pimples on her chin and her budding breasts sticking through the thin cotton of her dress. Crossing her arms in front of her chest and placing her hand over her chin, she sat, without speaking, for what seemed a long time. After a while, he wiped his eyes on his sleeve and looked at her. *You're growing up to be pretty, Miss Olive Grove.*

After he left town, she'd realised pretty quickly that the time they'd spent together in those three weeks between his father being hospitalised following his heart attack and his mother flinging the door open on them the day before his father's funeral hadn't meant anywhere near as much to him as it had to her. She'd felt stupid and dirty, realising that fact. She'd taken her father's thrashings and her mother's cold-shoulder treatment, refused to cry in front of them. She spent hour upon hour cooped up in her room, ashamed to come out, but defiant. She remained adamant that she was not lying. She took the story to her teacher, to the police station, and even to her classmates. *Someone* should believe in Roberto, and in her. But they weren't prepared to hear it.

Her own mother could not even look at her as she told Olive that they were ashamed of her, more deeply ashamed than she could ever understand. She'd wanted to hurt them, then – to challenge them. *More ashamed than when you thought I hurt Petey?* But she clammed up, stayed out of their way, not caring too much that they thought her a dirty little girl.

Nobody but Hazel listened, and she sometimes thought that Hazel pretended to believe her. She had nothing to be ashamed of; she was in love. And one day, Roberto Giovanni would be back for her.

She'd gone back to the store the day after finding him crying and smoking on the back step. They'd closed the shop for a few days. Mrs Giovanni was at the hospital, waiting for Mr Giovanni to die. That was when Roberto told her what had happened. He couldn't feel love, he said, he couldn't feel anything. He wasn't crying because his father was dying but because he was *still alive*, and *he might not die*. As he detailed all the things his father had done to him, Olive had cried, too. She could bear the fact of her father forever punishing her for what had happened to Petey, but it tore at her insides to think that a father could be so despicable as Roberto's had been.

Before she knew it, he was comforting her. He knew about her little brother, and the accident. The whole town did. It was that kind of place. She said then that they had blamed her. But the truth was that she and Petey were playing hide-and-seek and her dad had fallen asleep for ages and Petey had disappeared. Kissing her tears gently, Roberto'd told her that fathers were no good. They lied. She'd pulled away, startled by his kisses. It was okay, he'd told her. He said that he felt nothing. He was only comforting her. She'd cried more then. She'd never been comforted by a boy before. She felt strange inside. But she thought she liked it.

He'd tried again. Now it was his turn to be comforted. He kissed her more firmly and told her that he felt a little bit better.

She went back the next day, suggesting to her mother that the poor Giovannis needed more food so Mrs Giovanni could sit by her husband's bedside all day.

Within a week, he'd started to tell Olive that maybe he could feel something, after all. And after another week of gentle persuasion, the day before his father's funeral, she allowed him to discover that he could indeed feel love.

That day before he'd left, Mrs Giovanni had found them, entwined in one another's arms. They hadn't even done anything more than cuddle and kiss when she'd burst in. Her husband lay mute in the front room, his best suit stretched over his elephantine belly, his bulk crammed into the hastily constructed coffin. Mrs Giovanni rushed at her son, flailing her arms and grabbing at his hair, screaming that Olive, *the trollop*, was trouble. That he must stay away from her type. Olive had squealed and sat up, pressing her back into the wall, her arms instinctively rising to wrap around her head. She'd stayed that way, horrified by the filthy accusations coming from Mrs Giovanni's mouth, willing Roberto to speak up, to tell the truth, to defend himself, and her, against the vitriol. She didn't even know what those words meant. But he'd remained silent, allowed his mother to think the worst of her, and of him, and that night, while his mother ranted and raved at Olive's mother, labelling her daughter every name under the sun, he'd disappeared, leaving Olive in the middle of the mess.

Friday afternoon, second last period. Miss Jones tells the class what they must study for Monday's mid-year exam. Olive looks at Miss Jones, feigning attentiveness, but instead of jotting down notes she doodles in her notebook. Although she knows to the very day how long it has been, she counts the weeks on her fingers. Eight weeks have passed since the Anzac weekend. Eight weeks since he came back and left alone. She's as weary today as she was by the end of that day.

They'd been awkward with one another. He was back, he said, from Sydney, to arrange for his mother's transfer to the rest home. He couldn't stay, not with the stigma that still surrounded him following his departure. *You didn't do me any favours saying that*, he'd said. *People here have memories like elephants.* She'd thought of his dead father then, his dirty huge belly practically oozing out of the coffin, and started to protest. He'd put his finger to his lip, shooshed her like a little child.

She has never felt more alone than now. Even Hazel has abandoned her after almost seventeen years of friendship, turning her back on Olive, choosing instead to believe what Paul Carmody said he saw Olive doing at the railway siding just hours after she had tried to lure him away from Hazel with promises of kisses and something unspeakably dirty.

Olive is aware of Hazel's eyes boring into the side of her head, sending loathing and bile at her through space. She thinks about writing her a note, telling it all exactly as it was, letting her know that she did not do those things that Paul Carmody said she'd done. Instead, she sets her jaw tight and draws a heart, writes *Natalie and James forever* inside it and viciously crosses it out.

Nervous being with him, she'd lit another cigarette. He'd reached out his hand and taken hers, moved to the edge of the bag, and pulled her down to sit beside him. Her nose brushed against his hair. She'd felt an urge to snuggle into it, to inhale the distinctive barbershop scent of the Brylcreem – and to feel his arms around her. He'd smiled at her, and she'd looked to the ground. *I knew you'd come back*, she'd said. *I'm sorry I got you in trouble.* They sat, not speaking. She could feel him looking at her as she stared at the ground. Her face burned and her breath caught in her chest as she'd tried to relax. He'd released her hand and lifted her face so she had no choice but to look at him. He'd kissed her. *I thought of you*, he said, after a while passed. *Every day.* He'd pointed back at the doorway of the old station manager's office. *Shall we go somewhere more private?*

Afterwards, she'd felt empty and sad. But she hoped he'd ask her to go with him, to the city. Instead, he'd asked, *What do you like to do nowadays? Other than paint yourself up like a streetwalker and torment hormonal teenagers?*

She'd noticed then, looking at him with his tightened face and the faint lines around his eyes and mouth, that he was a man, not a boy.

She'd stared into his dark eyes, and felt sick as she stated what she'd started to suspect within days of his leaving, and now knew to be the truth. *You lied.*

It wasn't hard to sneak a few extra clothes out of the house before school. The mornings are cold, and for the past two weeks she's been wearing gloves and a scarf, as well as an extra jumper over her uniform to keep warm. Her schoolbag is crammed full, and all day she's kept a close watch over it. Now she is supposed to be in after-school detention for leaving all her required books at home.

Behind the shelter sheds, she lines her eyelids in heavy black kohl before crossing the road and walking straight past the bus. She looks into the distance, avoids Hazel avoiding her.

She'd held it inside, wanting to speak to her parents after the Anzac weekend, but only managing to find the courage last week. She'd tried to explain running into Roberto Giovanni. Tried to explain her shame and embarrassment at having been lied to, and taken advantage of. She'd felt the pain of her father's disciplinary measures that day as he whacked her with his belt. *This one is for Mr Giovanni and the slur on his fine reputation.* Whack. *This one is for Mrs Giovanni and the early grave you are sending her to.* Whack. *This one is for your mother.* Whack. *This one is for me.* Whack. *And this one...* Whack. *This one is for the teachers and police, and everyone else you lied to.*

When he was done, she stood trembling, her legs shredded with pain. She looked him in the eye. *Your pants are falling down, you stupid, pathetic bastard. Give yourself a few now, for the lies you told that day Petey drowned. You think Mum doesn't know you were passed out drunk?*

She passes the cemetery and old people's home. She's heading for the highway. Never coming back. Near the railway siding, she pauses and rests her bag. By the time word gets to the farm, with luck she'll be on her way across the Nullarbor. She unwraps the scarf and removes her gloves, peels off her school jumper and checks to make sure she's alone before pulling her school dress over her head. Opening the bag, she reaches in and pulls out her mother's precious green dress. It's too big and smells of mothballs, but once she pulls a cardigan on and buttons it up, she imagines she looks like a slightly younger version of Natalie Wood.

Leaving her school dress and jumper neatly folded on the bench and walking towards the highway, she practises her spiel for the truck driver who'll hopefully stop before one of the townsfolk sees her. *Hello, thank you for stopping. I'm Natalie. My car broke down in that dreadful little town and I have to return to Sydney before my university examinations.* The smell of mothballs is already less overpowering. By the time she reaches Sydney, the stench is sure to have faded.

1972–73

Ned's daughter

There's a gap before she sighs. I've never seen a whole body sigh before. Moving warily across the room, I sit down on the vinyl-covered kitchen chair. She looks up, rests the iron in the wire stand and sighs again.

'Whaddaya mean, exactly?'

'A dad, have I got one?'

She turns away. It's rude. But I say nothing.

'Yeah, you have. Well, you did…He died.'

'What's his name?'

She picks up the iron and spits on her finger, sizzling it onto the metal plate, and resumes ironing my school dress. 'Jesus, Elvira-Louise, you ask a lot of bloody questions for a nine-year-old.'

It took several days – a long drive across a dry and dirty country – to get to this house. We didn't stop much, only for food and petrol. And when she got too tired to think straight, she'd pull off the road behind some bushes and sleep on the front seat.

The same twelve songs played over and over in the tape deck. Sometimes she sang along. I discovered pretty quickly that I could annoy her by asking when Gran and Granda were coming to get me from her house. She'd look into the rear-vision mirror, and grip the steering wheel tighter when I asked. I needed to cry, but she'd made it clear that it wouldn't change things. So I told myself not to, over and over. I made annoying her into a game. But it was no fun for either of us. I'd ask her the same question every time the man in the tape sang about writing the letter to the postman. I'd use my whiniest voice, too. *When are they coming for me?*

The first time I asked it when that song came on, she laughed. The next time, she looked into the mirror, met my glare and raised her eyebrows. I turned away. The time after that, she said I was a *smart little turd*, and I was *pushing all her buttons*. She sounded pleased when she said it, though, and I felt a bit like I did when Granda paid me compliments using his outside language.

Natalie uses outside language constantly, inside and out. Not long after we'd arrived at her house and I started school, the new teacher, Mrs Ramsay, made me stand in front of the class and pointed out my shabby clothes. I was an example of what not to be. After school, I asked Natalie to wash and press my school clothes for me. She was less concerned, it seemed, at being told that I was feral than she was by my use of one of Gran's airs and graces. *It's an iron, Elvira-Louise, not a fucking press.* She walked to the kitchen and came back with the jug cord held in her two hands. She folded it so the metal parts were together and, holding on to them, she whopped the jug cord across the back of my legs. *Next time,* she said, *you'll remember the difference between a* [whop] *fucking iron and a* [whop] *fucking press.*

She hugged me then. *Sorry, sorry, sorry.* She was stiff, and waiting for me to pull away. She told me that the man with the silly name – Gonzo – wasn't coming back again. She liked him, she said, and thought he'd come good in time. Though I hardly ever saw him, I hated him. He'd mostly visit her when I was asleep, or pretending to be asleep. She told me once that he couldn't cope with her having a kid. It made him uneasy, me being around. She was using lots of

Granda's outside words. I was happy that he wasn't coming back but didn't say it. He had crazy-eyes, just like the man from home who'd stand outside the shops in town and yell at the shopkeepers to unlock the doors and let him in.

I decided that while she was hugging me and saying *sorry, sorry, sorry*, I would try and tell her that I didn't know how to be Elvira-Louise. Maybe in the times before I could remember, when I was a baby and had lived with her, she'd called me that name. But for as long as I could recollect, everybody had called me Loulie. Granda hated the name Elvira, and I told her what he said: that it sounded like the name of someone who tortured puppies and kittens for fun. That amused her, and as she repeated it back several times she softened and the next hug was not a guilty hug. I thought about Gran missing me, and pulled away from her. She said that Loulie was an ugly name. But after that, it's what she mostly called me.

I sit on the chair across from her and walk the stupid Sindy doll up one of my legs and down the other. She'd given me the doll the first night we were here, wrapped up in pink paper with a big bow. I am too old for dolls and hadn't even played with them when I wasn't too old. But I didn't say that. Instead, I did as I had been taught by Gran. I thanked her politely and found something nice to say about the doll and played with it sometimes while she was around.

I make Sindy pirouette on my toes, over and over again, thinking: I am still eight. Not nine. I force Sindy's legs into the splits.

Natalie sighs with her whole body again. Maybe she heard my thoughts and she feels sad for not knowing how many birthdays she's missed while she was somewhere else.

I pull Sindy's legs together and sit her on my lap, stroking her hair. Natalie puts the iron down after a little while and tells me to look at her.

'You are going to have to get used to people treating you like you are shit. People think they're better than us. Next time someone asks you that, tell them that his name is…or was…Ned. Just Ned.'

She moves across the room towards me and laughs as though she's said something funny. She's all high-pitched and cackling. She kneels down close to me so that her long, dark hair brushes against my eyes. Too close now, she breathes deeply and sucks some of my air, and breathes the taste of rotten ashtray into my mouth. I remember collecting the ashtrays at the pub and taking them outside to the big metal bins out the back. They hadn't smelled anywhere near as bad as this, but Leslie and I got paid fifty cents each for doing a dirty job. Then Granda would slip more money into Leslie's hand and give us a wink. 'Time for you kids to go outside and play now, eh?'

Natalie clasps my arm with her red talons. I try not to flinch. She likes me to hold her hand and call her *Mum* in front of people. But now we are alone, I can call her Natalie inside my head and avoid calling her anything at all out loud.

I try to shrink smaller in the chair as she lets go of my arm, and grabs my chin and shifts it so that I am looking into her eyes. 'His name was Ned. Ned – bloody Ned Kelly. Satisfied?'

There is to be a trip soon, the week after I turn nine. We will go on a bus ride to Pentridge Prison, to see where they used to hang people to die, and then go to the Botanical Gardens for lunch. I am excited about the picnic. I want Natalie to put her name down to be a mother-helper. She can't come. She has to go to work because if she doesn't look after us, then nobody will. She has to make sure that the new machine takes the peas out of their shells properly before they go into plastic bags and into the freezer. I think about those peas, still in their shells, pouring into bags by themselves and spilling onto the floor if Natalie isn't there. I don't care. Stupid people can take their own peas out of shells. At home, on the farm, we'd never even *seen* such a thing as peas in bags.

I beg her to come. I even call her Mum. I don't say that I want to show everyone that my mum is real because she'll ask why, and then she'll go on and on again about people thinking we are no good.

Before I came here, I didn't even know that I was no good.

'Elvira-Louise, I bloody can't. Who do ya think pays for all this?'

She waves her hands around the room, which is so higgledy-piggledy and messy with piled-up dirty clothes and pizza boxes that I feel overwhelmed and hopeless just looking at it. I miss my spick-and-span Pine-O-Cleen home. And I miss Gran's constant reminders that my shoes don't belong *there*, and my chair won't push itself in. Here, I can throw things on the floor any old place if I want to. But I don't want to.

Natalie gives me her hard-faced stare. I'm not scared of her now. She's loud and makes lots of threats, but she can rarely be bothered carrying any of them through. I haven't felt the jug cord around my legs since the day I put on airs and graces, and I think that hurt her more than me, anyway.

'I'll tell you who, Missy. Not fucking Ned, that's for certain.'

Ned gets the blame for everything around here. Sometimes she laughs when she blames him for us having no money, for her feeling sick from drinking too much, and even for me being born. She tells me that I can't tell anybody who Ned bloody Kelly is. It is our secret. But it's too late for that. When Mrs Ramsay told the class about Ned Kelly's armour, I called out loudly that Ned Kelly was my dad. Everyone laughed at that, even Mrs Ramsay. *If you have got a father with that name*, she said, *then he's probably got the same bad blood as the original Ned Kelly*. By the time the bell rang at the end of the day, a chant, *Loulie Liar, pants on fire, daddy hanging on a wire,* followed me out the classroom door.

I dawdled, collecting my bag and coat. After the others left, Bobby Snider pushed me up against the bag hooks so my skull squashed into the pointy part. *You haven't even got a real mum – only a witch.*

On the day of the trip to the prison to see where they hung people to die by their necks, I want to stay home. I say that I don't even care about the stupid picnic anymore. I'm almost crying. We used to go on picnics all of the time at home, sometimes just me and Gran and Granda, and sometimes with other people when we had the whole town race and picnic day. But I'm not old enough to stay here by myself without nosy people interfering in our business, and Mum has to pay for the roof over our heads.

The bus trundles along the road and the class grows louder and more unruly with each passing mile. I wait for the ugly chant to start, but the class has moved on to *Smelly Kelly, smells like rotten jelly*. She's sitting on the seat next to me and looks at me like maybe I can save her. She is going to cry and I feel sad for her, but I push her off the seat on to the floor and turn away. Bobby Snider laughs and grins at me, but I don't feel good.

We get there, and once we're off the bus we line up in two straight rows. We promise to be a credit to our teacher, and to our school. We forward march one two, one two, and hal–t. Mrs Ramsay points to a large sign: *This way to Ned Kelly's Armour*. I am crying. I can't stop – it gets louder and louder – I haven't let myself cry like this since I watched Gran and Granda through the back of the car window, waving, shrinking and then disappearing as the dust from the car tyres erased them.

Mrs Ramsay reaches into her handbag and roughly shoves a stiff-with-old-lady-snot hanky into my hand and tells me to stop being stupid. Felicity's mum tries to be nice and gives me a hug but it makes everything worse than ever. A man, who tells us he doesn't get paid but loves the prison so much he became a volunteer tour guide when they closed it, leads us single file into a room called the gallows, talking all the while. Mrs Ramsay glares at me. I can't stop the tears, though now I am weeping silently and trying to suck globs of snot into the back of my throat as quietly as I am able to. The man points to the exact spot where Ned Kelly stood before they snapped his neck and he went to hell. He says that the dark marks on the wooden floor may have been made by Ned Kelly's own blood. I put one hand to my throat. When we are allowed to walk around and look but not touch, I quietly tell the man that my mother says that our life is hell on earth. I ask if Ned Kelly is in the same hell on earth, or if his is different. I have to repeat the question, and Bobby Snider and Timothy hear and put their hands around one another's throats.

The man, who has a tattoo under one of his eyes, smiles, but not as though he is laughing at me for having a dad with the same name as the bushranger.

'Ned Kelly died long before you were born, kid. Way before.'

He must think I'm stupid. I knew that already.

'Ned Kelly was a bad man,' says Mrs Ramsay. 'Let that be a warning to you all.'

Mrs Ramsay makes me walk to the bus behind the other children. I am not to speak, not even a single, solitary word, until we get back to school. And I am not allowed off the bus for the picnic. I must pay for being a troublemaker.

I draw Mum's hair so it is black and long enough to sit on. I make her red fingernails as long as swords so she can fight away all the bad people. I write *MUM* and draw love hearts and stars all around it so it looks a bit like Granda's tattoo. When art time is finished, I put my hand up fastest and go to the front of the room to show my picture to the class. Afterwards, when Mrs Ramsay tells me to sit down, I go back to my desk nicely but I say *don't shit and piss with my mum* inside my head and smile at her without using my eyes.

The day after the prison trip, Mum left the peas to fall over the floor for one hour, stomped into the classroom in the middle of reading time and called Mrs Ramsay an *evil little bully*. She still had her hair tucked into her hairnet, but I didn't even care. She said that she'd wipe that nasty fucking look off Mrs Ramsay's face if she ever tried it again. At school now, everyone wants to play with me and Kelly. But we don't let them. Not unless we need people to hold the ropes for skipping.

Before she came to get me, Mum was in love with the man who couldn't cope with her having me. He thought he could. Then he met me and every time he saw my face he realised that he couldn't stand the thought of Mum loving with another man. She tells me these stories at bedtime. I'd much rather have a story from a book, like the one about the sad little prince that was Gran's favourite when she was a little girl. But I know Mum is trying her hardest, so I don't complain. She curls up next to me at bedtime and tells me about how she met Gonzo before he went away to the war that we sometimes watch on the news at teatime. He was different then. When they went to the Royal Easter Show, he won her the big brown teddy bear that sits on her bed. That was the day she told him about me. She'd cried when she told him and he promised to help her get me back. If she speaks for long enough, her sour-sweet grapey breath soothes me to sleep. Sometimes she shows me photos and reads out little bits of letters Gonzo sent from the war with Charlie, but only the bits that are suitable for my ears. We were going to be a family together. But he came back from the war with an angry and broken brain.

Mum is on the couch, watching a plane fill up with soldiers. The big door closes behind them. Some men smile and give a thumbs-up or two-finger peace sign to the camera. Others look really tired and try to smile but can't quite manage it. She says they're sending them home and 'that's that, we're leaving the goddamn fucking war'. She's crying and saying 'what a waste' over and over. Her eyes are bloodshot and puffed up like squishy overripe tomatoes. She's blotchy and has bitten her nails and scraped off most of the polish so it looks like splotches of blood all over her fingertips. She sends me to have a bath, and I take as long as I can because I already know.

    I get out and tiptoe to the lounge room. The sound has been turned down, so all I see are flashes of images from our teatime viewing. She's still on the couch, but now she's asleep. I go to her room and drop my towel and stand naked in front of the mirror like she sometimes does. I pinch and squeeze at my skin, sigh with all my body and pull a sad face at myself. I pull on her knee-high boots. They come nearly all the way up my legs. I paint my eyelids bright blue and silver and carefully blink into the mascara wand to make big black eyelashes. I outline my lips fire-engine red, going over the edges until my mouth is surrounded by a red heart from my nose to chin. I lean forward and stare at my eyes in the mirror, purse my lips and step back to admire the effect. Not taking my eyes from my reflection, I make a jagged lipstick scar from one side of my stomach to the other, just like the one Mum still has from me being ripped from her screaming body nine and a half years ago.

Through the mirror, I see her at the bedroom door. Our eyes lock. She doesn't raise her eyebrows, or do anything except stand rigid, arms crossed. For the past few weeks, ever since they told her that they didn't want the likes of her at the factory, she's barely left the couch. And since I watched the men getting on the plane, I've known that soon she'd say what has been coming since the day I waved to Gran and Granda until they were erased. But first she says that she's hopeless, that it is too hard, that she is not made for a life alone, and that she is not even good for shelling peas for a living. I listen to her and I feel sad for her, having to say those words about herself. But as she rubs cold cream into my face and tells me not to open my eyes while she rubs off the make-up, I try not to smile too big with my painted mouth. I am thinking about all those soldiers, going home.

1974

Naming

Neither of them had had any experience with a human birth before that day. It wasn't done back then for a father to be anywhere near the birthing business. But who else was there? Just the two of them. Stuck on the farm, three weeks before the due date. No way in or out, middle of a flood. Once the shock of it had worn off, he'd felt special. Not too many blokes were there at the beginning like that. And there was no doubting the connection he'd felt with both Evie and baby Olive after that.

'I said, what do you dream about?'

He's still thinking of her mother when Loulie asks that. Had him wrapped around her little finger from the outset. He'd thought back then that he'd always take her side, even though he loved her mum more than life itself.

She shifts from foot to foot. Scraggly yellow hair tumbles free from its clips. Hands on bony hips. Chin jutting forwards. Fixes him with that challenging gaze. Just like her mum used to do.

He doesn't know what he's supposed to say. Feed her a lie? Spin sugar and spice? Tell her the truth – that something that he thought was fixed has broken again? Confess that he's as weak as piss?

NAMING

In the nick of time, Evie saves him. Comes to the door and calls the kid out of the bedroom. Looks at him. Disappointment all over her face. Like he's the one thing standing between her and happiness.

She tells the kid she needs a hand to collect the eggs. He thinks she's going to leave him to his ruminations but she demands he get out of bed. Now! She stares him down and tells him, loudly enough for the kid to hear, to set an example. For less than a moment, he sees himself giving her a walloping. Showing her that, despite all appearances, he's still the boss around here. Not that he really would. Never had no time for any bloke who rules his missus with force.

The back screen door bangs shut after them. He drags himself out of bed, stretches the cricks out of his legs and back and gets washed up. Puts on his good strides. Digs out the kid's favourite shirt – the one her gran wrapped up for her to give him for Christmas back she was five. Gives himself a good talking-to. Plenty of blokes had a worse run than him and got through without succumbing to plonk to numb the pain. His old man'd be ashamed if he were here. Teetotaller all his life. Mad as a cut snake, but seemed as fit as the proverbial mallee bull right until the end.

He's out on the verandah, pulling his boots on, when the kid turns around and sees him. Gives him a cautious half-grin and wave. Tugs at her gran's sleeve. Points back at him. Evie gets on with it. No pomp or fanfare. No eyebrow raises or knowing looks from her. The useless old prick has got himself up and outta bed. Big deal. About bloody time, she'll be thinkin'.

A few minutes later, they come out of the chook house. The kid glances up and sees him still there, leaning against the apple tree. No need to let on that he's got a touch of the morning-after shakes. When she comes across the yard – as she's bound to any second now – he hopes he'll be able to stand upright without his knees giving way. Her face lights up. She's walking over to him. That heart wrench again. It's Olive he's seeing – as she was – cheeky, full of the potential for mischief.

He gives her a wink. 'Hey, sport. Wanta go into town for ice-cream?'

She looks back at her gran. The kid knows who's really the boss. 'Both of you, I mean.'

Evie looks at him, suspicious like. He expects she's thinking that for the past month she's been left to do it all around here – settle the kid back into a routine, deal with the day-to-day running of the farm, cook, clean, feed 'em all – while he goes off on another bender. She's biting her tongue. Probably thinkin' she's got as much time for driving into town for ice-cream as she has for sitting around the hairdresser's like those Lady Muck townies.

'Get ya hair done, too, while we're there.'

She softens, just a bit.

They're sitting on the bench at the municipal park. A poodle's trying to mate with a kelpie. Evie'd have a conniption if she came out of the hairdresser's and saw him just letting it happen in front of the kid's eyes. But what the kid hasn't seen on the farm before – cats, dogs, sheep, all at it like rabbits – probably hasn't been done. The kid looks up and grins. Wrinkles up her nose. Points to the dogs and teases. 'Wait till I tell Gran about that.' Waits for his response. Slides in closer for a cuddle.

He's clammy and his gut is turning cartwheels. He wishes the kid hadn't talked him into an ice-cream cone of his own. He's trying to work out how to get rid of it when the Mulligan boy shows up out of the blue. Got built-in radar, that one. The kid shoves her dripping cone into his hand, runs across the park and grabs at the boy's arm, just as he reaches the edge of the playground. Dragging him in the opposite direction, she starts yacking away, a mile a minute, like she's picking up a conversation she left just minutes ago.

They used to talk about it sometimes, him and Evie, about the funny sort of bond the two kids had formed since that first time Olive turned up at home with her. Six months old, she was. Scrawny as an orphaned lamb in a drought. The poor mite screamed the nights away. When Olive bailed in the middle of those nights a week after she came back, Evie'd taken the baby into town for a check-up, and the Mulligan kid took a shine to her in the waiting room.

She walks across to the other side of the park, yabbering away, and he can't help thinking about standing there that day her mum came and took her the last time. He knew, watching the car disappear, dust rising in its wake, that this time was going to be different. Olive wasn't going to be bringing her back, saying she couldn't cope, after a couple of weeks. It takes some kind of determination to drive across the country by yourself to collect a kid. He should've said something to Olive then. Cleared the air a bit. Showed her he thought she'd done good to sort herself out. But his heart was ripping, thinking of little Loulie goin' away forever. Tore at his guts, seeing the kid kneeling on the back seat, staring out the back at them. He'd reached over to Evie, tried to pull her close. Like he used to before their life went to buggery. She pulled away. *You truly are a stubborn bastard, Len.*

Through all the ups and downs, the dark and the light days combined, that's one thing she'd never done. Sworn, like that.

You coulda stopped 'em, she said.

Left him out there, alone, leaning on his cane, staring as the dust cloud grew, then disappeared. Walked into the house without turning back to give him even a glance. She was right. Would've taken just a couple of carefully chosen words to Olive. Evie didn't talk to him all that night. Or the next day, either. She kept looking like she wanted to spit something at him but had decided he wasn't worth the effort, after all.

He wonders if the kid's telling the Mulligan boy about her time with her mother. He isn't too sure, really, if he even wants to know what happened over there. Whatever it was, she talks about Olive like she's some kinda superhero. Never mentions the stuff that's killing her mother's brain cells, rotting her teeth, taking away her life and her looks.

Two days after they'd been called, they were off to the city. Borrowed Jonesy's sedan and off they went. Got lost about three times, trying to get to the airport. Made it with five minutes to spare.

Got to fly on a plane by herself with a big cardboard tag pinned to her chest. Looked like she was going bounce out of her own skin, coming off the plane, and seeing him and Evie there, all dressed up in their best city clobber. They were both sure as eggs trying not to think about what it really meant to have her sent back again – alone, this time. Wasn't even taken to the airport by her mother.

Walking down that blue carpet, next to the air hostess, the kid had rushed ahead as soon as she spotted them and hurled herself at Evie. Got to eat sandwiches in sealed cellophane bags, she said. Wrapped her arm around his waist as they walked to the car and said quietly that she was *glad and sad* to be going home.

A couple of hours later, on the way back to the farm, it was clear that she'd faded. Looking back at her in the mirror, he could see a cloud had come over her. And her eyes, when they met his, had that shadowy look that he keeps seeing since she's been back.

Out of the blue, that first night they brought her back, when the kid was finally asleep, Evie had wanted to go over it all again. What had *really* happened all those years back when she was in the hospital? Knocked him for six, it did. He wanted to tell Evie to leave it be and that he hadn't stopped loving their girl – ever – no matter what she'd done. But he'd clammed up. Took off to the shed, saying he had something urgent he needed to fix, couldn't wait until morning. Scrabbled about under the workbench, looking for his medicinal bottle. Didn't even bother wiping off the dust. Fell off the wagon, again.

She *knew* what happened. He'd gone over it in minute detail. Recounted it over and over. He'd turned his back for no more than two minutes. Rested his eyes for one. He'd timed it over and over in those first months when nobody was around. Stood at the apple tree. Looked down at his watch. Waited for the second hand to reach twelve and started walking. He'd kept going into the kitchen. Took the bottle from the top cupboard. Pretended to have a couple of quick swigs. Then put the bottle back. Doubled the forty-five seconds it took to get from the apple tree to the kitchen. Two minutes. Two and a half minutes, tops. That's all he was gone.

He didn't worry when he'd come out. Not at first. He expected that the cheeky buggers were playing a trick on him. He sat down at the base of the apple tree and waited for 'em to jump out from behind him and give him a scare. Closed his eyes. Just for a second. Waited for them to grow bored and come back. Dozed with the sun on him. No longer than a minute. He was sure of that. Jolted himself awake and there was Olive, standing in front of him, looking down and smiling like butter wouldn't melt in her mouth.

Where's Petey? Still hiding, is he?

He was knackered. Running the farm and wrangling two kids were knocking the stuffing out of him. If only he'd listened to Evie, let her call for help from her interfering do-gooder sister while she was in hospital. Too damn proud to admit that his Evie was a bloody workhorse, far more capable than him. That was his trouble. Evie'd tried to warn him. But he was too bloody stubborn to listen.

Going to be weeks before I can do anything much around here, love. And you'll miss your weekend in the city.

He'd miss the trip this once, he'd told her. She was much more important than any get-together with the boys. He'd manage with the kids. Ensure Evie got a good rest at home once all the things causing the women's problems were removed.

C'mon, Evie, remember who delivered Olive? I reckon after that, I can handle anything.

She'd laughed at that. Looked at him as though he was clueless. But gave in.

Olive stood there that day. Just looking down at him at the base of the tree. Said nothing. Not a word.

He'd grown uneasy. Felt a chill shudder through him. Pulled himself up and told her to take him to where she was hiding her brother. *What's going on? Enough's enough. Where is he?*

The kid comes back with the Mulligan boy, tells him she's thirsty. Someone's jammed a stick into the water fountain and they can't get it out. Can he come and help? The poodle's tailing the kids. The kelpie's gone home.

He pulls himself up, throws the soggy ice-cream cones to the poodle. Wipes his hands on the back of his strides. Remembers they're not his work pants and tries to unwipe them.

'He's from Mrs Smith's, from the butcher's,' she says. Wiggles her fingers to entice the dirty little powder puff over to her. 'Can we take him to her?'

He nods. Groans. 'Bit bloody hot out here in the park, anyway. How about we drop in to the RSL on the way back for a glass of lemonade? Your gran'll be ages yet.'

The kid looks at him. There's a sparkle in her eyes. She knows that once they're inside, he'll spring for a plate of hot chips without too much coercion. Glancing across at the Mulligan boy, she grins like the cat that got the cream.

'Whaddaya think? Reckon your mum'll mind?'

He reaches for the kid's hand. Waves the boy over with the free hand.

'C'mon. We'll keep it a secret, eh?'

Knows full well that Evie'll hit the roof if she hears he's taken the kids into the RSL without her. Christ knows what she thinks'll happen without her there to supervise.

The kids run ahead, dragging the dog. She's unthreaded the tie from the waist of her dress and turned it into a makeshift lead. Reaching the butcher's, they go in and hand over the dog. He waits outside, thinks about the cool beer that he's just minutes away from. Just the one, he'll have. Take the edge off. Then they'll pop back to the park and Evie'll be none the wiser.

He leans against the glass. Taps his cane on the window to give the kids a hurry-along. The kid is giggling. Telling Joe's ma about the recent antics of the dog, no doubt. Wicked sense of humour, that one, just like her mum used to have at the same age. Not that he'd ever given the poor kid much to laugh about. The Mulligan kid is standing there, torn between giving in to his need to laugh, and behaving respectably in front of him and Mrs Smith. The kids reach out to take a slice of polony from the end of a long pronged fork. He watches them thank Joe's ma and turn and pour out of the door, Loulie still yabbering a mile a minute.

It was the silence that had given her away. That made him know for sure that she was hiding something. From the moment he pulled her, resisting all the way, out of her mother's body, Olive had barely stopped making a fuss and noise. She was a kid born needing to be noticed. Lived every moment of her life like she was on the stage. Could talk the leg off a chair, that one. But from the moment he snapped open his eyes that day and their eyes met, she'd said nothing. Not a single bloody word.

He tore through the property, looking in all the sheds, calling Petey's name. Promised him lollies, a visit to his mum in the hospital, a new bike, even. He yelled himself hoarse, and at one point grabbed Olive and hoisted her off the ground. Screamed in her face: *Where is he?* Knew somehow that he'd not be finding their boy anytime soon.

He thought briefly about the dam, a good five-minute walk for an adult, over the hill. Dismissed the idea. He'd been away two minutes tops – rested his eyes for no more than thirty seconds. He ran to the house. Petey must've followed him inside. Probably walked straight past him while he took a sneaky swig, then, exhausted after a morning outdoors, fell sleep in a heap on the bedroom floor.

Loulie wants to drop Leslie home. His dad'll be hours yet at the meatworks and it's too far for him to walk. She tells him he'll have to jump in the back like a dog, and she goes to jump in there, too. But he knows Evie'll have none of that.

Before he's even had time to compliment Evie, to tell her that she looks just like she did on the day they'd met, she's got the kids scrunching up together in the front. He looks across at her and smiles as the old ute starts first time and he gives the dashboard a pat.

'Our trusty steed never lets us down.' He winks across at his wife. 'You look beautiful, Evelyn Justine.'

And she does. Sitting in that salon with half the town gossips for the past two hours has done wonders for lifting the tension from her face. He jokes that maybe he should go in for a colour and set, too. Take a few years off his tired old husk of a body. And he realises as he says it that he's been a stupid bastard, that the grog will lead to nothing but more pain and misery for them all, in the long haul. And Christ knows, they've all had enough suffering for a dozen lifetimes, surely?

The boy laughs when he says Evie's name. Pokes Loulie in the ribs. 'Your gran's got a funny name like yours.'

'Loulie's not funny. Neither's Louise.' She pinches the tender skin over his ribs.

'No, stupid, your real name.'

The cloudy look comes over her again. She bites her lip. Looks up at her gran and away. Talks to the windscreen. Quietly says that her mum wanted to call her Evelyn Louise but didn't want Gran to think that she wasn't still mad at her for sending her away with a baby growin' in her guts.

'Called me Elvira instead, from a film Gran used ta love.'

He feels the energy shifting. Doesn't want to enjoy it. Wouldn't be right. But he's relieved to have some of the pressure off. Doesn't feel like he's on probation anymore. None of us is perfect. That's the truth of the matter. Though he's not about to say it out loud.

The boy knows when to shut up. Perceptive little bugger. Starts telling them instead that they're going up near Perth for two weeks after Christmas. Going to stay in a caravan again.

Evie reaches across and gives Leslie's arm a bit of a squeeze. Smiles at him. Tells him he's a lovely boy – a credit to his parents. Tries to blink the tears away from the edges of her eyes before he notices 'em. Avoids turning to her right and meeting his.

They pass the cemetery, and he tries to lighten the mood.

'Dead centre of town, kids.'

As they drive parallel to the perimeter fence, the kids are holding their breath. Olive used to do the same thing. He wonders where they learn this stuff. Checking his mirror, he pulls over. Leaves the car idling on the side of the road for a few moments.

'I wonder how long youse are gunna be able to last.'

He pulls back out on the road as they laugh and gasp for air at about the same time.

'Hate to tell you this but ya can't catch death germs from in there.'

He looks over to Evie as they pass the oldies' home. She's staring straight ahead. He lifts his left hand from the wheel and points back at the cemetery. 'Make sure you send me straight there, with no stop-over, love. Got no desire to spend me days sitting around, waiting for the move next door.'

They're having a cup of tea and fruitcake. Loulie's gone to bed. Looking forward to being dropped at the Mulligans' to play tomorrow afternoon. He's about to raise what Loulie'd said in the car, but changes his mind.

'Heard a whisper today that it's only a matter of time before they shut up shop altogether out at the meatworks. Reckon there'll be none of them left in work soon.'

Evie looks across at him. The Evie he saw for those few minutes after she came out of the hairdresser's is gone. Tucked away somewhere inside the tired and sad version of herself.

He doesn't want to make her any unhappier. Been enough of that.

'Just worked out why the Mulligans go there for their holidays,' he says. 'There's still a tannery and fertiliser factory there, isn't there? I reckon that he works and the wife and kids get to have a summer holiday. Good bloke, that one.'

In his head, he's convinced that Olive was guilty of something that day. He'd never quite worked out what, though. A kid doesn't just clam up like that for nothing. There was no way, his rational mind would tell him, that a girl could hide a little boy so well that an almost week-long search party could find no trace. But he could tell, from the shifty way she'd looked at him, that she'd been up to no good. That was before he would admit out loud that something was terribly wrong. Before he'd called for help, he gave her the first walloping of her life. Demanding, as the stick he'd stripped from the apple tree came down on her backside, that she tell him the truth. Begged her, with tears pouring down his face, to be honest. Swore that he'd stop if she'd just own up to what she'd done. She stayed quiet the whole time. Refused to cry. When he was done, he'd grabbed her by the shoulder. Tossed her to the ground and went in to call for help. Couldn't ever trust her after that.

'I knew that.' Evie takes a sip of tea, lifts the pot. Asks if he'd like more.

'Why not? Tea for me from now on…and don't worry, love. We'll do the best we can for the little one. She'll be all right with us.'

1976

The light

This time she's scared them. They've never got the police involved before.

She tosses a coin. Heads, north. Tails, cross back over the Nullarbor. Try and catch Gonzo and make things right.

Tails.

Maybe she'd be better off seeing who pulls in to refuel? Who'll take pity on her and offer her a lift? Might be that she can't be fussy, anyway. That she'll have to let fate decide.

Better if someone heading north offers her a lift. Gonzo, the bastard, doesn't want to be caught. Wouldn't have dumped her here with a hundred bucks and the clothes she's standing in if he had. Could have at least left her backpack. Not that it had much in it. She left most of it behind on her father's driveway as they sped off ahead of the cops.

A bit later she practises her breathing. Tries to keep the anxiety at bay. Like she'd been shown in the hospital. But the kid keeps creeping into her head in the quiet spaces. The hospital. Who's she trying to fool? Say it like it is. She hadn't known they'd been told. Not until Len'd said it. Quiet. Almost under his breath. Like the anger had finally drained out of him.

Look who's here. The jailbird.

The kid was behind him. Didn't recognise her for a second, she was so tall. The old chenille dressing-gown had just about set her off crying. When she'd seen it, she'd wanted to say, *Christ, Mum, you still have that old thing?* Had an urge to pull her close so she could feel it brushing on her skin. But she hadn't. She was too intent on getting the kid's attention. Wanted her to see that it was all right, that she'd just come to say hello. The kid moved then, and stood next to her gran. She could tell, even then, that she'd already picked her side. Staring at her, she was, a sullen expression on her face.

She knew then it was never going to work. She'd started crying, and saying as much. Then idiot Gonzo'd left the bike and stormed across the front lawn. Started shoving at Len. Still wearing his helmet. And Len, he just took it. Wouldn't let 'em set foot in the house, no matter what she said. Reckoned he could tell they were out of it. Said that they were going to get a court order to keep her away from all of them. *Not a fit mother.* And Evelyn, well, some mother she was. She'd let him go on running her down in front of her own kid. Even though she hadn't been perfect herself, and knew it.

She'd screamed. Called 'em every name under the sun. By then, Louise was screaming, too: *Go away. Leave us alone!* And then Gonzo had to go and fucking punch Len. Right in front of Louise like that. Dumb cunt.

She's sitting under the lean-to about fifty metres from the bowsers when the panel van pulls in. Must be close to dawn. When the driver gets out, he's all lit up by the roadhouse spotlights. Probably no more than her age, but he moves like he's an old man. Bad back, or maybe he's just driven for hours. Shoulders are drooped. She watches him open the van and shuffle stuff about in the back. Pulls out a sheet and shakes a pile of dirt into the air. Takes a couple of jerry cans and, once they're filled, heaves them into the back. Then he pauses for ages, like he's thinking. Closes the back door. Slams it shut so hard that the old geezer inside the roadhouse peeks his head out. Wondering, like her, no doubt, if he's about to do a runner. The driver reaches into the van, scrabbles about and pulls something out. Leans on the bonnet and scribbles on a sheet of paper. Stuffs it into an envelope. Goes inside.

He comes out after about ten minutes, drinking from a bottle of Coke and carrying the letter. Goes to the postbox and looks up the road as though expecting a red postie van to pull up and collect it. Guzzles his Coke down. Throws the bottle in the bin. Burps. Stands over the bins and rips the letter into a heap of small pieces not much bigger than wedding confetti. Walks back towards the car. He looks harmless enough, so she moves closer.

'Room for a freeloader?'

She's standing by the passenger door now, hand over her mouth and her face turned so he can't see her straight on.

'Give you some money, if you want.'

Not too much of a talker, just enough not to be creepy. That suits her. Says he spent his adolescence shifting stock and setting up cattle yards in remote northern and central Australia. She doesn't say she spent hers on the streets of the Cross and St Kilda.

They've been on the road for the best part of the day when he turns off the highway. She hadn't expected that. They'd stopped every so often to refill the tank from the jerry cans and to drink dusty water from the canteen he kept lashed to the roo bar on the front of his car. Sometime around the middle of the day, he'd pulled in to a roadhouse and bought them both steak burgers and hot greasy chips and Coke after refuelling the car and cans. She parted with five dollars and took a shower in red, stinking, metallic bore water. Brushed her teeth with the same water and the flat of her index finger. Wasn't sure if she felt better or not after she'd put her undies on inside out, and pulled her sweaty jeans and singlet back on.

For a while the car bumps over the corrugated road, and she's worried that he may be intending to harm her. Could be anyone. Maybe this is what her fate is to be. That'd be right. First smart decision she'd made in years, so she'd thought, was to tell Gonzo to fuck off when they'd pulled up to refuel. Ironic if she ends up dead after that.

Her old man was a bastard, but as they'd roared out of town on the bike she knew she couldn't abide the thought of another night with someone who'd hurt a near enough to one-legged old man in front of a kid. When Len fell to the ground, she'd jumped on Gonzo's back. Started pulling at his neck. Tried to drag him away. She'd discovered in those moments that she had certain standards and principles that must've been obscured for all those years. It was hopeless even trying to talk her way inside the house after that. She'd brought her trouble to their door. Broken one of Len's cardinal rules.

She put on her helmet and grabbed the bag she'd opened a few moments earlier. After Len opened the door and saw her there, she'd half emptied it, to try and show the kid the drawing she'd held on to for all this time. Thought it might be proof enough for Len and Evelyn. But with Len on the ground and Evelyn screaming at her to go before she called the police, she'd known there was no point. She'd broken her parole; she wasn't going back inside. She got on the back of the bike and they left, leaving the upturned contents of her bag on the driveway.

Must be half an hour that passes before she notices there's an expanse of dark sheen out towards the horizon and something glimmering an orangey colour. Mustn't be too far from the coast. The glow reminds her of something Gonzo once told her about a light that hovered in central Queensland. Could have been aliens, or ghosts. Promised her, just two days before talking her into heading west before she was cleared to go, that he'd take her there to see it – and the kid, too, if she really had her heart set on them trying to be like a family. Said he'd sell his bike – buy a car – if that's what it took for her to trust he meant it this time.

Mangroves edge the waterline. He doesn't speak as he follows the corrugated track through a gully into a low-lying rugged and jarring range. She thinks of the poem they used to recite at school. All sunburn and sweeping ranges. *Should be singing that as our anthem,* Len used to say, *not singing praises to England's bloody gracious Queen.*

He turns off onto another jarring track and pulls up at the base of an imposing mound of smooth boulders. Turns the engine off and sits there. Staring ahead. He looks miserable. Deep inside himself.

'You goin' ta kill me now or something?' She's nervous. The sky's burning orange and the sun's starting to go down. 'Don't even know your name. And I'm as thirsty as buggery.'

That seems to jolt him out of it. 'Don't be stupid. Too hot for that.'

He grins at her and she relaxes a bit. He still looks sad – and a bit mad, too – but not threatening.

'Just going to get out and get some more water from the back. Don't panic. I haven't got a gun in there.'

He winks and opens the car door. He's sort of handsome but not in that tough, swaggering way that Gonzo is.

She gets out, too. Looking around, she's struck by the way the rough and craggy-edged rocks seem to coexist with weathered smooth boulders. How they seem to be at the same time randomly and deliberately assembled in mounds, plateaus and stunted ranges in the midst of this sea of low-growing scrub and spinifex. She thinks of saying how weird that it looks unnatural but is as natural as you can get. But the air is oppressive, oxygen-sapping and bone-bleaching hot, and she saves her words.

She gulps down a couple of mouthfuls of warm, dusty water from the plastic bottle he passes her. Who'da thought dirt and water could taste so good?

He walks away a few metres, stretches his arms over his head and arches his back to lengthen out the driving cricks. She thinks of Gonzo, and the acrobatics and moaning and groaning he'd do about his aching back and hips each time he got off the bike to rest. Yet if she'd so much as winced, he'd be calling her soft.

When they'd pulled up at that roadhouse to fill up the bike, she'd told him she couldn't do it no more, and he'd thought at first that she was joking. When he realised she'd meant it, he closed-fist punched her in the face and dragged her by the hair across the car park of the roadhouse and forced her to sit down on the edge of the gutter. Reaching into his pocket, he threw some crumpled notes at her. *Try and do it without me, then, you useless slag.* In his other hand, he held a great hank of her hair and he'd looked at it and sneered before shaking his hand so it fell to the ground. Then, brushing his hand on his jeans, he'd turned and strode back to the bike, taking off moments later. How long had she sat there before the old geezer had finally come out? Could have been minutes. Or hours. *Don't want no trouble*, he'd said. *It's just me here. One old man.* Gave her a pie and a bottle of juice in a brown paper bag. Said it was best she got moving as soon as she could. When she reached into the bag to pull out the juice, she saw he'd wrapped twenty bucks around it and secured it with a rubber band.

'Whaddaya think? Beaut here, eh?' He's finished stretching and is standing next to her. She likes the gentle tone of his voice. She passes the water bottle to him.

She thinks she can smell the ocean. Hear it, too, off in the distance. Not breaking rhythmically on the shoreline. But crashing. She visualises it, violently thundering into a rock-hard cliff face. Smashing aggressively. A fist into a face. Her face. Her father's face. She thinks of Louise – the horror in her eyes as Gonzo punched her grandfather to the ground. She'd wanted to protect him then. Realised in the second of seeing the kid's eyes that violence, was alien to her now. She'd forgotten she hated the old man. *I'm sorry, Dad*, she'd cried. Tried to help him up. But he shook her away. She knew she had to leave. No good could come of her being around.

He walks back to the car. Reaches in through the open driver's side window and pulls the keys from the ignition. She tenses. Wants to say that she might be plenty of other things but she's no thief. But she doesn't. Pocketing the car keys, he indicates with a tilt of his head for her to follow him.

She shrugs. Grins. 'Okay, as you don't plan to kill me.'

She tries to maintain the grin, but the whole left side of her face hurts like crazy.

They pass around the outcrop of boulders and follow a trail a couple of hundred metres through the scrub towards the crashing sound, stopping at the base of a shell midden. He tells her he's seen something a bit like this before, in Queensland and the Territory, when he was trying to be a drover. She wonders if he saw that light, too.

'Those ones were heaps smaller, though, near old creeks and rivers. Think they must've been partly washed away, by floods or something. Nothing like this one. You could walk up this if you wanted to.'

She wonders if he's waiting for her to say something. So far she's revealed nothing. And he hasn't asked her a single question. She supposes the old geezer back in the roadhouse must've said something, though. She'd noticed him flinch when a pack of bikers came roaring up behind the van earlier in the day and overtook them.

He doesn't say anything else for a while. Stands there, reaching up and touching the weathered shells halfway up the mound.

'Reckon these must've been here for thousands of years – the lower ones, anyway.'

They are close enough to the water for her to feel the salt stinging around the edges of her smashed-up nose. Reaching out to touch the midden, mirroring his movement, she then brings her fingers to her nose, flinching as she brushes the tender, swollen skin. She says that she fancies she can still smell the remnants of the seafood meals once consumed there.

'No.' He smiles at her. 'That's just the blood inside your pulpy nose.'

She shifts back a few steps to try and take in the scale of the rubbish heap of discarded shellfish remains. Tries to imagine how many people were fed at how many gatherings. Hundreds? Thousands? And how many stories and lies were hidden within the mound? Still moving backwards, she scratches her exposed shoulders against a clump of scrubby acacia and swears.

He's moved away and is squatting on his heels under the scattered shade cast by a paperbark.

'You've been here before?' she asks, moving towards him, realising as the words come out that of course he must know the place. How else would he have known to turn off the road and follow the track, veering off where there were no signposts?

Easing herself down to a flat rock close to his side, she looks towards the sound of the crashing. When she concentrates, it seems to echo off the rocks. Perhaps he'll lead her through there. Past the midden, further into the bush, to see what lies beyond the squiggly rough path wedged between two low cliff walls – to witness firsthand the power of those smashing waves. She's never had religion, but there's something soothing and spiritual-like about being here, and she feels close to relaxed, sitting there with the sun disappearing while the intense orange sky turns purple and grey.

He reaches for her right hand and shakes it. 'Excuse the bad manners. Don't think I've introduced myself. Paul.'

She clasps his hand. 'Natalie.'

She supposes this is the part where she tells him about herself. So far she's remained tight-lipped when he's said those few things about himself that she expects were aimed at drawing something out of her.

'I took these classes once,' she starts, 'in social behaviour. You wouldn't think a person would need to learn that, would you?' She doesn't say that the classes were taken while she was inside. 'I passed. Guess I'm considered acceptable now – by some.'

She'd been optimistic when they let her out early. She'd kept her head down inside and done all the courses they'd offered. Trained up in office work, too. She had a plan. And she'd put in an application, so as soon as they transferred her to a new parole officer, she'd go back to the west. Get established in a job and make a home for her and Louise. A proper job this time – with prospects – and she'd go see her parents. Show them she'd changed. Hadn't counted on Gonzo rocking up, though. Thought she'd purged herself of her need to be with him.

'It's only you what's got to think you're acceptable – to start with, anyway. Reckon you probably don't right now.'

THE LIGHT

When she was little, her dad sometimes used to have a quiet presence, a bit like Paul's. She'd been too young, at first, to work out that when he was like that, it didn't mean he was sick of her and her chatter. He'd grown distant from his family. But he'd usually manage to hold himself together, and draw on that quietness to settle her down. She remembers how she'd be always on the go – always wanting to do something, inventing games, imagining, putting on plays and impromptu dance recitals – always the shining star, the centre of her dad's universe, even when he felt real bad. *Chatter, chatter, chatter.* He'd grin and drop his shoulders, giving an exaggerated sigh. *Come on, kiddo, let's go outside and have some quiet time before Petey wakes up from his nap.* And he'd haul himself up from his chair, using his cane for leverage, and lead the way out the back. Get her out there on the pretext of watching for birds come to eat from the trees in the house garden. Pose some kind of question for her to consider while they watched the birds. *Can't speak. Not even a whisper or they'll fly away.* Didn't take long for her to work out that it was just a ruse to stop her talking for a few minutes.

After Petey disappeared, a lot of things stopped. Not just her chattering and imagining.

Now, for the first time in ages, she wants to talk and talk some more about all the things she's had bottled up inside since leaving prison.

'I read this book…once.' She realises she'd been about to reveal where she's been. 'About how once a woman has a baby, she becomes riveted to it, or something. And then she grows weak and allows herself to be open to domination – from men.'

'And that's how you came to be…?' He points at his own nose.

'Not exactly. Tell you the truth, I didn't really understand the book properly. But I keep thinking about it. Maybe it was me trying to get away from domination that led to this.'

She touches her own face. Shows him her mouth, pulls her lips back and shows him the gaps where there used to be three teeth.

'Never gunna win first prize in no beauty contest, eh?'

There'd been other books, filled with complicated ideas about feminism. And there were women who'd claimed to be inside just for protesting for equal rights. Radical, angry women who'd scared her with their passion. Told her she had entitlements. That Louise was her kid. She didn't need no man, the kid needed her mother, grandparents should keep their nose out of her affairs, Gough'd see her right. None of it made much sense to her.

She didn't know where she'd belonged, inside. Not with them, but not with the good women, the housewives and mothers, either. What she'd done to both Louise and to that first baby ensured that. Since running away from home as a teenager, she'd tried to find her place. In those first weeks out of home, she'd gone through a lot. Swallowing her pride and seeking assistance from characters her father would have described as shady, at the very least. Had to ask a stranger where she could get help. Waited on a side street to be picked up and taken to the doctor. The blindfold they'd insisted on was frightening enough. Supposed to be protecting her, they'd said. Reckoned it could save her from getting charged if the cops got wind of what she'd been up to. Terrified after being shoved into the back of a car and driven to that place, where she'd endured the most excruciating and humiliating physical pain of her short life. Unceremoniously dumped by the roadside afterwards. Bleeding. Agonising. Wanted her mum, more than ever. So far as she could tell, there was little that might be considered conventional about her life since then. She'd vowed never to do that to an unborn baby again. And she hadn't. Although it wasn't enough, she'd tried her best the second time she fell pregnant. And despite spending more time away from the girl her baby had grown into than with her, she feels as though a part of her *is* riveted tight. Like she's still connected and there's an invisible umbilical cord.

'Seems to me,' she says, tilting her mind back to the present, 'that maybe the oppressed ones aren't just the housewives and mothers. It's bloody hard for everyone.'

She slaps at a midge on her arm. 'Fuck. They're brutal, aren't they?'

It's dark by the time they reach the highway. They hadn't spoken much. She'd asked about seeing the waters crashing into the cliff. *Too dangerous at night*, he'd said. *Maybe some other time we can come back. In the daylight.* She liked the feeling that gave her. Something to do. Another day. In the future. An option, maybe? Then he'd told her that more than a hundred years ago they'd forced a bunch of women and kids off the edge of that cliff face. *Took the men. Put them in chains. Made slaves of them.* And she was glad he hadn't taken her there.

She'd been on roo watch on the way back to the main road. Took her role seriously, pressing her forehead to the dusty windscreen and scouting the terrain. She'd been amazed at the way they'd been thick until night fell properly and then had vanished into the darkness.

'I had a brother,' she says after a while. 'He was sweet and perfect and my mother was obsessed with everything about him. It was like she lived only for him. Dad and I didn't mind, because she left us alone to be loud and silly and get into all kinds of mischief. And then he went and disappeared and that was that.'

She hadn't told Gonzo about Petey. On and off for all those years, and she'd kept all her secrets – all the defining stuff that made her into what she was – close to her chest. What passed for a relationship was always focused around him and his needs, anyway. Placating his rages. Tiptoeing about his moods. But when he was being nice, there was something special about the man.

'What do you mean *disappeared*?'

She'd barely been aware of speaking aloud, of telling her most shameful mystery to a near stranger.

'Just that,' she says. 'Wandered off when he was a toddler. Found him five or six days later…in the neighbours' dam. They said I took him there.'

Inside, she'd eventually told the psych that she'd been blamed. That she really didn't know to that day whether she'd done something or not. And how, when having her own baby proved too difficult to manage, with no man and no money, and when her thoughts turned dark and she'd been fearful of what she might do, she'd returned to the farm with the baby, and tried to put things right with her mother. *What exactly were you trying to put right?* the psych had asked. She couldn't answer. Was it her mother's loss of her precious son? Or something unspeakable – something that the child she was may or may not have done? She doesn't want to be in that space now. It's nice, sitting here next to Paul, the hot night air blowing in her face, watching the white lines flash by under the glare of the spotlights. Tensing up as the road trains pass every so often and whoosh the car so it feels for a second or two like they're going to be run off the road.

'That's enough of me. What's north, for you?'

He doesn't say anything for a long time. Stares straight ahead, but still concentrating on the periphery. Looking for roos. And cattle.

'If you must know, I was planning a one-way trip. A disappearing act of me own.'

She remembers that long pause he made after pulling in and refuelling, before he picked her up. And the letter, too, torn into confetti and dropped in the bin. Maybe, like her, he was on the run from something – a woman, probably.

'So what changed your mind?'

'Wasn't sure that I had changed my mind at all. Until I sat under that tree back there.'

'What was the letter you ripped up? A break-up note?'

'Something like that. The old codger back there said you needed help, urgent like. My timing was out.'

They continue in silence for a while before it dawns on her.

'I hope you're not going back there by yourself after you drop me somewhere?'

1980

Diseased

I go in alone and half expect to be told that Marion was right, I am a malingerer. Gran waits outside in the car. *You have the right to privacy*, she'd said, actually meaning that, with my history, I have no rights at all. That she'll find out, anyway, if I dare try to hide anything.

There's nobody else there and I go straight in. Doc Wilson leans forward. 'You know what they call this disease, don't you?'

His breath is rank. Like the pub bathroom before I've sloshed the disinfectant and buckets of hot water over it at the end of the night.

'They call it the Kissing Disease.'

He laughs, pleased with himself and his ability to make a teenage girl squirm in his presence. I'm tempted to tell him it is only his stinking breath that makes me uncomfortable, but don't. He's actually quite nice. I smile and pretend to be amused by his attempt at humour.

He leans back and adjusts his glasses. The tone of his voice changes. Like he's suddenly remembered who I am and he's judging me.

'You'll need to rest,' he says. 'Get your grandmother to collect your work from school. No more work at the pub, and no more weekend shifts with your Gran for the rest of the term.'

I don't know what to say to that. If I don't pass my exams, I can never expect to get a decent job out of this town. And without earning money, how much longer will it be before I can go? He says then that if he sees me working down at the pub before I am well enough to go back to school, he'll have words with Johnno. I like old Johnno, even if Gran used to call him Granda's enabler. Now that Mavis's gone and his kids have moved to Perth, the town's drinkers are his only family. I nagged him to take me on and he finally gave in, even though there's hardly enough work to keep even him busy.

When we pull up at home, Marion's on the doorstep. She has to sit with her dress hiked up and legs spread wide to fit her gut. It's disgusting.

'Oh, for fuck's sake, is she actually serious? Why doesn't she just move in with us?'

'Language, please.' Gran slaps my arm. But now she's laughing, too. I enjoy the moment. We don't have many of those anymore. Then the happiness passes.

'Give her a break, Loulie, she's had a rough trot.'

She hasn't called me that in ages. I hadn't realised how much I'd missed hearing it until now. Gran thinks everyone's had a rough trot. Except for us. She refuses to feel sorry for herself, or us, and never says anything self-pitying about the twists and turns our lives have taken. I get out of my side of the car, grab a bag of shopping from the back seat and pass it to Marion, now off her fat arse and standing, wheezing, by the car like a loyal old dog that some kid has dressed in a vile green and orange floral kaftan.

'Been raiding Kamahl's wardrobe again, Marion?' I say, ignoring the look Gran shoots at me. 'Glandular fever,' I add. 'No mention of being a malingerer, *Doctor* Marion.' I look at her with the disdain she deserves.

That shuts her up before she's had a proper chance to start. She tries to be funny and puts her fingers up in front of her face like she's trying to ward off evil and backs away from my germs. Seeing I'm unimpressed, she shrugs her shoulders and smiles at me and tells me to go inside and put my feet up.

Gran looks at me, sort of hesitating, waiting, I expect, to see if I tell Marion not to tell me what to do. But really I can't be bothered wasting my limited energy on the slovenly cow.

Inside, I turn on the telly and lie on the couch. When I was little, I loved sitting up beside Gran as she watched *Days of Our Lives*, and imagined us living in big houses with lots of dramas and twists and turns to keep life interesting. For a while, I get lost in the lives of the Bradys. There's something comforting about the way that after a few cliffhangers, everything is neatly resolved. How even when people die, there's sometimes another explanation.

In the past, Gran has carried the way we don't quite fit into the town like some sort of badge of honour. I couldn't even begin to count how many times over the years she's gone on about how *we're not exactly outsiders*, but we don't *lower ourselves* by providing small-town minds with anything extra to gossip about. Although that's hardly been a success. We manage to provide plenty of fodder for the bush telegraph. Every one of us who is, or ever was, part of our family has said or done something to invite interest in the goings-on behind our walls. When it came to my turn to be the topic of discussion, she told me not to be ashamed of my mistakes, but to keep our personal business our own business. That was the main reason I stormed out of the room yesterday when I heard Gran telling Marion that I was going to see Doc Wilson. Hearing that made me wonder what else she's revealed.

Our life is hardly the stuff of *Days of Our Lives*, but Marion's would make an even more ordinary TV show. She turned up in town with one suitcase and the clothes on her back, nothing else. Brazenly walked up to the front doors of the oldies' home and asked for a job. Told everyone who asked that she'd crawled out of one of the backwater coalmining towns after her husband left her for a twenty-year-old barmaid. I'd be ashamed of that, try to lose weight or have some pride in what I wore, or something, so people would stop saying it was no wonder she was turfed out. But she's not. The minute she arrives, she sits her fat arse down at the kitchen table and moans about what a useless prick he was and how the little slut is welcome to him and his pencil dick. The only time she's not moaning is when she's speculating about the lives of people in town or in the home, or prattling about the people in those stupid magazines she brings around for Gran to read once she's done with them. It gives me a bit of a pang to think of how Gran used to laugh with Granda at the same magazines. *Who cares about the shenanigans of Princess Margaret?* she'd ask after returning to the farm from one of her occasional treat days at the hairdresser's. *Nothing but gossip and fashion, and the latest D–I–V–O–R–C–E,* Granda would add, as if spelling out the letters gave him immunity from becoming a statistic. Now Gran reads the magazines from cover to cover and acts like she knows the royals and movie stars on a personal basis.

Over the past week, the two of them have spent hours dissecting every scrap of information they can find about the woman from Ayers Rock. Gran usually changes the subject if she thinks I can hear. First they believed the woman did something to her baby. Then they decided that no woman could do that to her own baby. They reckon that today they'll unearth the truth once and for all and leave no clue unexamined. As their voices become more impassioned, I'm stroking Lady Godiva's ears so hard that she yelps and moves away from me, turning her head to avoid meeting my eyes.

The sand trickles through the hourglass as the closing credits roll across the screen. Lady Godiva leaves the room without so much as a backward glance. I cross the room and snap off the television and the room goes quiet at the same moment they proclaim the woman guilty beyond doubt.

'After all,' Marion says, 'she didn't cry, and she dressed her baby in black.'

I can't believe what I am hearing. I stare at them. There's a big long pause and they both start giggling. They must've popped out the back for a quick puff while I was watching telly. Gran thinks I don't know she's taken to doing that since fat Marion came along. Then Gran speaks.

'And doesn't the name have Satanic meaning?'

She's still giggling. Maybe if she wasn't my own grandmother, it would be funny to see old people carrying on that way.

I turn to her. 'What does that even *mean?*'

And for a moment the real Gran is back. She stands and straightens the pile of magazines on the table and reaches for the empty teacups.

'Gunna let the kid talk to you like that? I'd give her a bloody walloping,' says Marion.

Gran does nothing. Doesn't stand up for me, even though I'm sick. Stands there, fiddling with the rim of the cup. Not a word in my defence. I look her in the eye so she can see I'm ashamed of her, running off at the mouth like that. It's a turnaround, that's for sure, and I'm milking the moment. Her eyes are a bit glassy. She looks miserable and pathetic…and isolated, too. I've never even thought of that before. No wonder she's lapping up Marion's attention. She turns from my stare. Hurt. Like Lady Godiva had been just a few minutes earlier. I call for Lady Godiva, and make a fuss of her. Then I storm out, slamming the door behind me.

'You fucking bitch, Marion!' I yell through the screen door. 'Go and ruin someone else's life. We don't need you.'

Kim is the only one who has a clue about me hurting myself. She's new at the private school, too, and is the only sort-of friend I've got. One day I forgot myself and took my jumper off and she saw my arms. I tried to explain. Said that my brain is wired like a rogue tape player. Fast-forward. Rewind. Pause. Play. It takes me where I'd rather not go. *Where it goes is completely out of my control*, I'd said. I told her, too, that watching the blood ooze helps ease the pressure from inside. She wanted me to go up and see the school chaplain with her after that. But I cried, swore I wouldn't cut myself anymore. Made her promise not to betray me. I told her a little bit then – the truth about Granda, and about Gran raising me alone now because my mum didn't want me, about Marion barging in and introducing all her bad habits into Gran's life. Not the rest, though. I don't think I could ever tell anyone that.

As the back screen door slams shut behind me, my rewind button takes me back one month or so, to before I started missing so much school. I was in a bad mood and headed down to the creek, on my own. I passed a front fence where a little girl played on the step, brushing her wiry dog. She was singing a song about the colours of the rainbow and her sweet voice stopped me feeling quite so mad at everything. I paused by the loquat tree on the verge and thought of Leslie. We used to raid that tree when we were kids, back when Mr Ferris used to live there with the two women who were sisters and his wives, all at once. I get it now, but back then we didn't get why Granda winked liked that at Gran when he talked about Mr Ferris. A bare-chested man I'd never seen in town walked by then, and threw something over the fence, and for one crazy second I thought he was trying to hurt the little girl and I ran to the fence just in time to see the wiry dog race off with the inedible crusty end of a Chiko Roll. A girl who looked about my age came out. She was barefoot and had tinkling silver bells on both her ankles. Her hair hung in two thick, ropy plaits and she had a sarong tied above her boobs and I could tell she wasn't wearing a bra. She looked fierce, and demanded to know what I was doing to her kid. I said, *I'm doing nothing*, and pointed at the man walking up the road. *Oh, he's all right*, she said, all mysterious, and picked up the little girl and, planting loud, sloppy kisses all over her face, said, *I'm going to gobble you up*. I could see, now that she was close, that she was older than me, but not by that much. The little girl giggled and squealed, *Stop it, Mummy*, and blew a big raspberry over her mum's nose. She looked at me and said, *I'm this many*, and held up three fingers. My chest constricted and I had to hold in a gasp. I stood dumbly for a bit, and maybe just because I was still there the little girl's mother asked if I wanted to walk to the library with them for children's story time.

That night in bed, the skin on my arm was red and already turning purple. After I got to the creek, I'd climbed into one of the dumped old cars and pinched myself tight, trying to turn my feelings away from inside my head. I kept my promise to Kim. I didn't cut myself. Or make myself bleed. I was exhausted. It was Saturday the next day and I had to go in to work at the old people's home with Gran and wash up after the Waitful Dead. I thought that maybe if I'd gone to the library and got to know the girl and her mum, I would've felt better now. I thought of the little girl singing and traced my fingertips in circles over my already bruising arms. I didn't know that Kim would see them the next day after I finished work and give me an ultimatum. *See the chaplain, or I'll never speak to you again.* Or that she'd move on really quickly when I refused, and she'd make new friends who wouldn't hold her back.

My mum used to play this game when I was little. *Round and round the garden like a teddy bear.* I told Granda once about the memory of my mother leaning over my cot, tracing circles in my soft little palms, *one step, two step and tickle under...*her red-dyed hair falling into my mouth. I'd tried to suck the taste of hairspray from her hair and she'd laughed. *You can't remember that,* he'd said. *She left you here the first time when you were too little to remember. Nobody remembers being a baby. And babies don't know what hairspray is.*

I lie to Gran about feeling better. I keep thinking about the girl in Mr Ferris's old house. She's new in town, or if not, I've never seen her before. Until I am back at school, I can hardly expect Gran to allow me to go wandering around town, trying to get to know the new people who don't know about me. So long as I can get through that first half-hour before the bus comes with Gran watching, I can pretend that I have the energy to get through the days at school.

The hour-long bus ride into school is enough to make me want to crawl into a hole and never come out. The interminably long hours spent there, even worse. But I'd been the one who'd wanted to change schools and repeat the year I'd missed so much of. I'd convinced Gran that I'd benefit more from finishing my education in the all-girls school, far enough away from town to avoid whispers. Gran could barely afford it. I knew that when I begged her to let me go.

The graffiti the rich girls write about me on the toilet cubicle wall is always inaccurate, but not entirely removed from the truth. I'd managed to avoid swimming at the beginning of the school year, feigning migraines, until I'd really developed them and spent two weeks in bed, eyes closed, wishing I'd fall asleep forever. I'd known it would be near impossible to spend the rest of my life hiding, avoiding having to wear my bathers in front of other girls. The cruel purple lines that stretch across my thighs and belly are evidence that I am no good, and not like them. Luckily there's only one year after this one.

On the way home from school, I can barely keep my eyes open. The bus stops to let one of the Year 12s off at the edge of town. Some smart-arse has adjusted the sign again. When Leslie and I used to walk out here as kids, the sign used to say *Population 1100*. But since they closed the meatworks and the logging has finally stopped, it has been crossed out and amended five times. The last one was *789*. Someone's spray-painted the latest addition, *666*, and painted a devil's head over the town's name.

Just outside the cemetery, the bus drops me at the bottom of the hill. When we first moved here, I'd walk home from school with Leslie and we'd race to the new place halfway up the hill. Now, each step is an effort. I'm pretty sure it's not all physical.

Opening the front door, I step straight into the large room divided by the high bench that used to be the counter in the days when our new house was a petrol station and shop. I thought that it was Gran's rostered day off. But, blinking to adjust to the light inside, I see Gran is drinking a glass of white wine. Her face is flushed and her eyes are crinkly at the edges. Her nose is red, like she's been crying, or maybe laughing. She's loose and floppy, with one leg tucked under her and her saggy arm spread across the back of the lounge chair, almost touching Marion's neck. I smash my bag down loudly on the wide counter, for effect. I stare at Gran. Shake my head.

'You're pissed!' I scream at her. 'You disgust me!' And without waiting for a response, I storm towards my room, calling back over my shoulder, 'You look like Granda.'

I hardly ever go out, but I go to the footy oval on Friday night after the colts training session in case she's there with the older crowd. I hang around the edges and pretend that I don't care that all the girls are looking me up and down and ignoring me, and the boys are looking like they're wondering if they might be in with a chance.

If she were here, I could start a conversation. Ask her what it is like being a single mum, not that I even know for sure that she is. It won't actually alter anything, anyway. My head may be bonkers but I can't *actually* rewind time to change anything. I walk away from the main group, across to the metal barrier that stops dickheads from driving on to the oval and doing doughnuts. I sit down. The oval lights are still on. They leave them on all night on Friday and Saturday nights, hoping that teenagers will go home. But where else are they going to go? I hardly see anyone from my old school anymore and I barely recognise some of them. They all seem a bit different – taller and almost adult. I suppose I might look different to them, too. Someone hands me a Coke can that has been opened and mixed with bourbon. I don't want it but I reach for it and drink greedily, wanting to fit in, just for now.

David sits down next to me, pressing his cheek into the cool metal of the barrier. He's got stubble on his chin. I read in the paper that he's been to court, and is on a good behaviour bond. I don't know what to say. I don't think I've even talked to him since I was in primary school and we were both Gold House captains for the athletics season.

For what seems forever, all I hear is the sound of my heart thumping and the embarrassing gurgling of my stomach as the bourbon and Coke go down and eat into my stomach lining. It feels as though these seconds are precarious, that we are sitting on the edge of a cliff over a choppy ocean. I can inch backwards, away from the edge, and turn and walk home without saying or doing anything more. Or I can fall.

Any moment now, I suppose he'll try to hit on me. And because I don't know what else to do, I will go with him to the back of the change rooms. He'll start by sticking his tongue down my Kissing

Disease riddled throat, and before long his hands will go down the front of my Levi's. I'll make out that I am resisting but I'll let him do it. I drink more and try not to vomit into my mouth at the thought of what is coming. I'm stroking my palm. The teddy bear starts running *round and round and round and round*. Another story comes, a bear, a golliwog, racing *round and round* and turning into honey, or is it tar? He'll reach that point where he starts groaning and saying that I'm a cock tease and that I owe him. He'll want to stick it in me because he believes all the lies the others tell. If he's not too rough, maybe I'll give him a hand job instead and make him promise not to say anything. I look at him and wait for him to talk.

He says his old man just got remarried to a bitch, and he can't talk about it to anyone. He points at the circle of teenagers five or six metres away.

'They don't get it,' he says. 'They've all got perfect lives but still it's all about getting pissed and ripped. Nothing else matters for them.'

I lift the can and make a fake toast. 'To us, a pair of fine young upstanding citizens of our town.'

We sit for a bit and then I say, 'What do I know about dads? I don't even know who mine is. Some random guy my mother met and couldn't resist, so the story goes.'

She really did tell me that story when I was eight, along with others. I'd have preferred something from a book – Cinderella or Pinocchio – anything other than the stories of her sex life.

I grin at him. 'Could be someone in this town. Maybe even your dad. Hellooo, brother.'

He laughs and says, 'I like you, Louise Kelly. You make me laugh. But you really should like yourself a little bit more.'

He touches my wrist then, all scabby and streaky under the lights. I pull my sleeve down and grip it with my fingers. I want to cry. And then I am crying and I can see he feels bad. He touches my shoulder and looks inside me like nobody since Leslie has, and I know he can tell that I'm not as tough as I make out.

DISEASED

I tell him that I've got the Kissing Disease, and how I decided if he was going to try anything I'd have infected him. He punches my shoulder and calls me a moll, but not like he means it.

'Hey, remember when we were primary school house captains and we'd get the little kids spinning on the oval until they fell over?'

I stand and walk a few steps away. Cathy Perkinson is watching us and I see her nudge the girl she's with and point.

'C'mon,' I say, 'remember how it used to be almost as much fun as rolling down hills?'

He looks at me like I'm demented, and sneaks a peek at the bitches staring at us. I can see he wants to do it. I reach for his hand to help him up and see him look over at the others again. The smell of mull is wafting our way through the air.

'Fuck 'em,' I say. 'I dare you.'

He puts his can down on the ground and we start turning slowly. When he comes close, I tell him that my gran is turning into a stoner.

'She'll be out here one day, with the cool kids.'

We're getting the hang of it now and we start turning faster.

'Put your arms out,' he calls.

We're twisting and turning. We keep going until the world tilts and we fall, laughing and clutching the ground so we don't fall into it.

I sit up, with both hands on the grass for support. My stomach is still turning. I tell him then that I am leaving. As soon as I've got enough money I am out of here. 'Not finishing school.'

'Shame,' he says. 'We could've been mates.'

'We still can be,' I say. 'Until I go, anyway.'

I say that to prove it, I'll tell him something you can only tell a mate.

'I think,' I say, 'that maybe my gran is lonely and desperate for company and misses Granda so much that she's turning into a leso.'

He looks at me, like he's waiting for me to laugh. And I do, but not because I'm bullshitting. I really do think that might be true. I say that I wish Gran could meet someone nice to make her happy – someone who is not Marion, someone with a dick, for example. He's laughing, too, now.

He looks in my eyes and is about to say something serious just as my stomach explodes its contents all over his lumber-jacket and desert boots.

'Fuck!' he says when I finally stop. 'You've given me Kissing Disease, you filthy bitch.'

Everyone's looking over our way now and we're both crying and laughing.

1992

Happy Haven Holiday Park

It is time to get moving again. She's stagnating. Happy Haven Holiday Park, this decrepit, rundown excuse for a retreat by the sea in the industrialised outskirts of Perth, certainly hasn't been much of a haven. Two years, and she is still under-employed and mostly invisible. She's weary of sitting up in bed night after night, attempting to close out the mistakes of her past, trying to visualise warm and fuzzy images inspired by the sound of the waves lapping faintly on the beach several hundred metres from her van. Where to go next, though? She'd got it so wrong last time – she'd relaxed and allowed herself to think she had found a place to belong.

She's mentally redrafting a letter of response to last week's letter, the second Karl has sent her since she'd shot through and made that ridiculous gesture. No apology, but an olive branch at the least. *Dear Karl, I am pleased to hear that your life is going so well. Yes, we did share some good times. I'm sorry I won't be able to make the trip north to visit you both this year, I am actually about to head to Europe.* Yes, she'll head overseas. She'll get a working visa for Dublin, or London, somewhere she can blend in and exist without drawing too much attention to herself. Come to think of it, maybe she can get citizenship, as Gran had been born somewhere over there.

Opening her eyes for just a moment, Louise thinks that at last, now that she's decided to leave, she can feel it – the ocean – soothing her. Realising it is just one of the newer park residents tapping rhythmically on the metal side of the van, she grows annoyed at being jolted from her decisive moment.

'Don't be afraid,' he says.

Pulling the oversized T-shirt she wears to bed over her thighs, she wiggles off the bed and stumbles in the half-light towards the window, grabs her manky cardigan off the back of the chair and drapes it over her shoulders. Winding the window open, she peers through the gap between the flyscreen and half-wound-out window and tells The Whisperer that she cannot help him, that she is alone. He should go to the caravan park office and ring the emergency bell if he has a problem. He ignores her. They *need* to go to hospital. They don't want to drag her out in the night. But they have no family, no friends. They are new here. Could she just watch their kid till they get back? A big ask but he is desperate and his wife won't leave until something has been organised. And to top it off, the car won't start.

'Please.' Then come the tears. Rolling down his face. 'We need you.'

The Whisperer leads her across the caravan park, past the toilet block and along the crumbling bluestone and asphalt path to the section this month's caretaker reserves for transients. He talks quietly the whole time with one of those one-tone modulated voices adopted by yoga teachers and meditation facilitators. She's straining to hear. They'd seen her, she thinks he says – on the beach just the other day – untangling a seagull caught in fishing line. She shows him the sore and festering fingers of her left hand, pecked repeatedly as she'd struggled to free the seagull. Though she doesn't say so, she's seen them about the park in recent weeks. She aims not to absorb too much of what goes on around her, tries not to let it get in. But the fluorescent pinks and oranges of his head wraps are as impossible to ignore as the happy family portrait the three, soon to be four, present.

She got into her car about two years back and removed the rear-view mirror. One hard yank was all that was required to separate it from the roof, where it had hung precariously from one loose screw. Leaving the mirror on top of the letterbox at the start of the three-kilometre red dirt driveway, she'd imagined Karl's perplexed look when he found it. Pushing the accelerator right to the floor on the corrugated gravel road, she'd laughed out loud as the car slid about and she momentarily lost control of the vehicle. By the time she reached the highway and turned south, she was pissed off with herself for her stupidity. The side mirrors were covered in a thick coating of red dust. By then she'd gone too far and she really couldn't look back.

The aerial had snapped off months earlier, so she'd travelled without any music on the car stereo, refusing to rest until the fatigue won. Once or twice leading up to those moments, she imagined herself taking one hand off the wheel, veering into the path of an oncoming road train, being done with it once and for all. A couple of times she stopped for a bit and pulled off the road, tried without success to sleep in a truck bay.

Bodily and brain-achingly tired for the last one hundred or so k's before hitting Geraldton, she drove with all the windows down so that the searingly hot wind blasted her senses. Sitting in the parked vehicle at an automated car wash on the fringes of town, she watched the brushes work through the layers of pindan red on her windscreen, jumping in her seat as the high-pressure jets of water switched on and sloughed through the pink-stained soapy froth. She thought then of that old Colgate ad on the telly when she was a kid. The teacher dips a stick of chalk into a glass of blue water, pulls it out and snaps the chalk in two. What was it that she'd said? *The plaque, it gets in.* Something like that. After leaving the car wash, she'd pulled in to the first motel she saw. In her homogeneous dank little room with dead-bolted window and a view of the skip bins, she'd draped a towel over the rust-flecked bathroom mirror and turned the shower on as hot as she could bear. Then she'd scrubbed and sloughed at her own pindan ingrained plaque layers.

After an adequate and unmemorable meal in the motel restaurant, she climbed in to the sagging bed. Pushing the highlights of the last slanging match she'd had with Karl out of her mind, she allowed herself to think of Leslie Mulligan, decided that the next morning she'd drive down and see if his boat was moored at the fishing harbour. Plotting the coincidental encounter – *Gosh, it has been…what, at least ten years?* – imagining the delight in his voice as he recounted the moment he'd first spotted her there, casually meandering among the fishing boats, she'd succumbed to sleep.

The child sleeps on a folded down table converted into a bed. Louise thinks of Leslie. He'd told her of sleeping on a table-bed in the same park when he'd come here before his dad left. Maybe it was the same van? As far as she recalled, the Mulligans had never had their own van, hiring instead the same caravan with a canvas annexe each year. The sheets never stayed on the vinyl mattresses, he'd said, and into the night he used to wake sweating and tangled in the sheets. She thinks he'd told her it was the last time they were here that he'd moved in to the annexe, and slept on an air mattress that went flat each night.

The little girl has a thick, luxurious mass of dark hair fanned out behind her head. Spread-eagled, she is draped in a faded blanket. Her skinny little arm sticks out, and in one hand she clutches a ratty flannel elephant. Louise allows herself to process this detail before looking around the shabby but immaculate caravan for somewhere to sit and absorb the events of the past five minutes.

Seated on the edge of the other bed, she focuses on breathing, counting on each inhalation and ensuring she exhales for approximately the same time. In and out, in and out, don't think, don't feel, don't think, don't feel. Two minutes before, she'd handed him the keys, whispered the quirks of the car – *no rear-vision mirror, no aerial, the doors don't lock, don't worry about that, let them take the wreck if they want it* – his hand on her cheek, then palms together, head bowed. *Thank you. Bless you. Namaste.* All bases covered. The Whisperer must surely have noticed the panic rise to the surface before he removed his hand and Louise stepped up the caravan step, careful to tread lightly and not rock the van and wake the child. His fingers, warm and alive on her face. How long has it been since anyone, other than Gran on her trips to see her, has raised a hand in kindness? She recalls the time when, after three interminably long weeks of the primary school Christmas holidays without her best friend to amuse and distract her, she'd nagged Gran to take Granda's patched-up old green ute and drop her at the bottom of Leslie's road. She'd walked up the hill to the Mulligan place. With each step, her excitement grew, so that by the time Leslie's mum opened the door she was beside herself and burst into tears when Mrs M reached down and hugged her. *We've all missed you, munchkin.*

A small tatty poster stuck on the wall of the caravan. A perplexed-looking chimp drops bananas in the toilet, a bubble from his mouth, *What happened?* Next to it a photo, slightly blurry, a snapshot of a laughing toddler on her dad's shoulders at the beach. The mother turns towards the child, a yellow kickboard in her hand. Rosie had a kickboard just like it. She'd spent hours lying on her tummy in the blue plastic, metal-framed wading pool on the verandah, arms outstretched, kicking her little legs while Louise watched from the nylon-webbed deckchair beside her. *Look at me, Loulie, watch me swimming.* Readying herself for the often-promised trip to the ocean.

The Whisperer's child sleeps messily and noisily. Occasionally she calls out garbled words. Louise tries not to intrude on the private world of the dreaming child. In the hour or so that she has been here, she has learned to breathe without counting. The child has thrown her blanket off, curled herself into a foetal ball and unrolled onto her back. Lulled by the child's rhythmic breathing, Louise wonders how the little girl will react when she wakes and sees a strange lady sitting on her mother and father's bed. Imagining the fear on the child's face, she forces the image from her mind, and stares instead at the orange floral cafe curtains over the tiny kitchenette. Orange daisies. In that last week there'd been daisies around the house in the Kimberley, tough bush daisies. Karl had surprised them, coming back from a trip to Broome with a crate full of hardy plants. *Look, girls, a garden, our own forest!* They'd rushed straight outside at Rosie's insistence and planted them immediately. Karl sat on the verandah, watching. Later, as they checked Rosie before going to bed themselves, he'd told Louise that he'd sorted things while in town. They had an extra week with Rosie.

On the way out of there, she'd pulled the daisies out, upturning them so that their roots wilted under the force of the forty-two degrees Celsius sun.

By morning, trying to find Leslie had seemed a bad idea. She'd decided to continue, as planned, and surprise her gran. She'd calculated that if she didn't stop too often, she'd be there by nightfall. But instead, after following a relatively short five or six hour drive, she'd checked in to the caravan park and was directed to an on-site van with a metal annexe stained with bore water. As she'd signed her name on the register, she'd had a sense of déjà vu, but at that point wasn't sure why. She'd told the guy with the torn and faded happy pants, and the smell of wet, mouldy wool emanating from his body, that she'd stay a week. After he'd shown her the van that was to become her temporary home, he'd run through the rules of the park: *no parties, no dirty washing to be left soaking in the ablution block sinks, empty your bins regularly into the correct receptacle*...Later, walking back past the amateur fishermen and women, stepping over their discarded blowfish, washed-up rubbish and beer bottles on the beach, she'd remembered the souvenir T-shirt that Mrs M had given her after one of their annual holidays. She'd forgotten that Happy Haven Holiday Park was the place that the Mulligans used to visit in summer. She'd heard so many stories about the caravan park. Crossing the neglected playground, with its rusting monkey bars and dangerously corroded slide, she'd paused as she reached the on-site family cabins and realised that, despite never having been here, she felt as though she somehow knew the basic layout.

After that first week passed, she figured she'd stay *just another*, then one more. Before she realised it, weeks had passed into a year. Then two years. And somehow she'd managed to exist without forming attachments. At some point, she'd acknowledged to herself that she had never actually intended going back home to see her grandmother. Maybe this had been where she was heading all along.

There is a message scribbled in marker on the fridge door. *There is no sense.* Louise contemplates it as she sits perched on the edge of The Whisperer's bed, resisting her need to leave the caravan and walk the hundred or so metres to the toilet block. She watches the sleeping child and attempts to see her without going back inside her own head. The Whisperer had pulled her close to him, *Just watch her until we get back*, before running off to be at his wife's side.

She'd been watching Rosie that day. Karl wasn't there. It had taken more than an hour for him to arrive after she'd called him on the two-way radio. He'd screamed at her over the radio. *Why the fuck did you call them? It was not your place!* It wasn't the time then to try and explain that she was trying to do the right thing, that she had wanted to break down the barrier and thank Ruth for allowing them the extra time with Rosie. How was she supposed to have known that he was pretending to have the dates confused? The time to try and explain, to make sense of the situation, didn't come until much later, when she'd been here almost twelve months and sent him that first letter.

After his ex-wife and the police officers had left with distraught Rosie, Karl hadn't run to Louise's side to seek or offer comfort. He'd been furious, dangerously so. Della had copped a Blundstone boot in the guts simply for being there. Running to stand between him and the cowering bitch, Louise challenged him to kick her, too, if it would make him feel better. She'd held her arms out to him then. But instead of accepting her embrace, he'd pulled away. *She is not yours. Don't interfere in our lives!* Grabbing the keys off the table by the back door, he'd stormed out.

The Whisperer's child kicks off her blanket and wriggles as though her legs are trying to run her off to the faraway places of her imagination. She scrunches her nose as her unruly dark hair tickles her and laughs out loud a bellowing hearty laugh of someone older than the five or so years that Louise guesses her to be. Resisting the urge to reach forward and wipe the hair from the face, to scoop up the child and draw her close and inhale, Louise stands and stretches from side to side.

They were out the back by the verandah, filling the paddling pool. Rosie, remembering her yellow kickboard back in the house, came running to her to tell her she was going inside to get it. Pulling her squirming little body close, Louise had inhaled deeply and sung: *sugar and spice, all things nice.* Rosie pulled away. She was on a mission. No time for indulging Louise. She ran in, and then back out. *Loulie, Loulie. There's my mummy and some mans at the front door.*

The Whisperer's child stirs, props herself on her elbows, and fixes Louise with a disconcerting gaze. She yawns and opens the conversation with a question. 'Do you like peanut butter?'

Standing by the door that day, holding it open, aware that in Karl's bitter and twisted mind she had betrayed him, she'd reached to Rosie and gently squeezed her arm. She'd thought then of her own baby, signed to someone else's care nearly thirteen years earlier. Did she, or would she ever, know Louise even existed?

The Whisperer's child wants more stories. *My daddy tells me lots of stories.* Louise opens the cereal box and pours a bowl of Weeties. She finds milk, sugar, spoon and her own voice, and begins a story. A stilted and stolen story. One of Leslie's stories. An awkward, wonky story of the *good old days, the better days, the days when life was drifty and dreamy.* Days when kids would help Dad pack up the car for the annual summer migration, panicked calls from the back seat when they set off: *Didja remember my lilo, my new bucket and spade,* and from the front, Mrs M, *my magazines?* The good old days, the better days, the days of tinned Spam and beetroot on white bread for lunch. Cricket on the radio. Beer (for Dad) and shandy (for Mum). Half tipsy, Mum'd be seated in her new Christmas terry towelling shortsuit on a striped deckchair. Dad making a production of meal preparation in his *Kiss the Cook* Christmas barbecue apron while the kids raced around in the near dark, pulling old ladies' undies off the line and hoisting them up the flagpole. She points, then, to the photo of the family, the little girl with the kickboard. She starts to tell of the fun they'd had, her and Rosie, planning a beach trip for the next time Rosie came to stay.

'I was her nanny,' she says. 'But I wanted more…'

And because she expects that she will never reveal herself to an adult with the story that she keeps locked inside, she tells another story, of a young woman, barely more than a child herself, gifting her own baby girl to a family who could give her all the kickboards, beach trips and peanut butter she'd ever desire. The Whisperer's child listens solemnly, then climbs into Louise's lap and rests her head against her chest.

'To a Queen and King?'

'Something like that.' Louise breathes deeply and allows herself to feel. 'I'm going away soon,' she adds quietly as the child reaches up and gently twirls her nose-ring. 'On a plane, across the sea, to begin my life.'

1999

Unsaid

Evelyn is exhausted. All that needs doing, now that she is home, is to open a can of cat food for Tinder. Then, while her shepherd's pie zaps in the microwave, she'll run a Radox bath to ease her weary old body into. Perhaps she'll put on a record and dim the lights in the bathroom. Maybe then, she'll be able to relax, and allow herself to think about nice memories for a bit before turning in for the night.

It had taken a few moments for her to recognise Leslie earlier, in the shop. As soon as she did, she'd wiped her hands on the front of her apron, and walked around to the front of the counter and pulled him close.

Of course I'm still here, you cheeky young whippersnapper, she said to his chest as she released him. *I might be old but I'm not ready to be put out to pasture just yet!*

Taking a step or two back, she held his large, roughened hands in her own and looked him up and down. Noted the greying at the temples, the lines around the eyes, the subtly receding hairline and softly barrelling belly.

The good life seems to be agreeing with you, young man.

Leslie grinned at her and patted his gut. *Yeah, that's one way of looking at it. Slowing down a bit. Nearly forty, can you believe it? Enjoying too much of Sil's good cooking. I tell you what, Mrs...Evelyn, never thought that I'd see the day when I turned into a fat bastard, but there ya go. Price you pay for marrying into an Italian family. It's all about the food, and the food.*

He turned at the sound of the door buzzer and waved a woman carrying a baby over. *Evelyn, this is my wife, Silvana. And our latest addition, Bianca.*

Silvana reached for Evelyn's hand and clasped it warmly. *I've heard a lot about you. I didn't know you worked here. Leslie didn't mention it.*

I forgot, he'd said. *To tell the truth, I figured by now you'd have your feet up and be resting. Shoulda known, eh?* He reached to take the baby from Silvana. *And we've got a boy, Lenny.*

Dropping his gaze from Evelyn's, he'd shuffled the weight between his feet subtly, moving from side to side. He could have been fifteen again, awkward, shy, seeking Evelyn's approval. She experienced a tug of tenderness.

A little boy. Nice...Lenny? She looked at Leslie, met his gaze and smiled. *Where is the little tacker?* She checked behind Silvana's back, as though a small child may have slipped in unnoticed while the adults were speaking.

Asleep out front in the car. Thank goodness. Silvana rolled her eyes and sighed. *Grizzled and moaned for the past two hours. Conked out just outside town – just as this one woke up. Typical of kids, eh!'*

Driving home three hours later, past the town cemetery and turning off to go up the hill towards her house, Evelyn'd felt fatigued. She'd been a bit shaken by Leslie appearing out of the blue like that. He'd been on her mind. Certain things had been weighing her down more than usual lately, and she'd been feeling the need to talk about them. Before it was too late.

All those years working in the old people's home had given her enough experience of the elderly to know that, for her age, she was unusually sharp and sprightly. But today, as well as her shaky mind, her feet and back had ached more than usual.

Leslie was probably right to be surprised at seeing her there on her stool behind the till. She was no spring chicken, and was certainly slowing down. Occasionally, she fancied that she and the town were sliding steadily into decrepitude together. Perhaps after her next overseas trip she'd think about quitting work.

Edging the Corona into the carport, she'd remembered that she hadn't been hungry the previous night after work, and had left in the fridge the shepherd's pie she'd prepared before her shift. Instead, she'd had a couple of crackers with cheddar cheese and Vegemite in front of the television. Out of the blue, she'd felt her mood slide, and sank into one of her rare periods of self-pity. She hadn't slept at all well after that, waking repeatedly through the night with bad dreams, and struggling to get back to sleep after each one. She recalled the dream of being observed, of eyes without faces tracking her movement through the house. And of voices calling for help, with increasing urgency.

Checking the mailbox and finding it empty, a wave of exhaustion had rode over her and imprinted heavily on her shoulders. She hadn't had a letter from Louise for close to a month, the longest she'd gone without receiving a thin aerogram envelope from her granddaughter since she'd left Australia.

Opening the front door and moving through the room, she'd then been struck by the number of possessions she'd accumulated in the years since Louise left the house. She doesn't remember ever deciding not to throw anything out, but it seemed that she'd turned into a collector of newspapers, magazines, broken crockery and discarded possessions picked up on her long walks around town. It occurred to her that perhaps she was seen now as eccentric, salvaging others' cast-offs like that.

In the kitchen, she'd reached down slowly to scratch between Tinder's ears, and moved to the tap to fill a glass with water. The kitchen wasn't much better than the living room. Hard to imagine she's the same person who'd thrown out just about everything except the record player Len'd purchased for her in the early seventies. No matter how angry she was, no matter how strong the desire to purge every trace of him throughout that period, she'd been unable to part with that.

As the bath fills, she reflects on the fact that more than twenty years have passed, but still she wonders if moving off the farm like that had been the thing that ultimately led to the undoing of Louise. She knows, with the benefit of hindsight, that she'd acted too hastily. All she could think to do was leave as quickly as possible – to physically remove herself and Louise from the place of all that pain – to try and start afresh. Making a snap decision to find something closer to town, a new roof over their heads, one without memories and sadness attached, became a matter of urgency. There'd been a couple of houses available in town at the time, but she knew she didn't want to be plonked smack bang in the middle of the fishbowl. As overwrought as she was, she'd managed to keep some degree of practicality. She'd have no income, at least until she found a job of some description. And she couldn't sell the farm until legal matters were sorted. She simply didn't know what the future held.

The house was decrepit and the rent dirt cheap. Hippie squatters had been there for a while throughout the period when Australian boys were first being sent off to Vietnam, and then it had sat abandoned for a couple of years. They'd removed the old underground tanks and bowsers before she signed the lease, and built a proper bathroom at one end of the hallway. But that was about the only concession made to convert the old petrol station and shop into a home. When she'd gone to look at the place, she'd considered telling the owners to leave the wall painted with anti-Vietnam War slogans and peace signs, imagined what a talking piece it would make if she ever invited anyone over. She'd chuckled, thinking of Len's reaction. He'd have had a conniption. He liked everything neat and tidy and in its place. And despite everything that had happened in his own time away, he'd felt Australians had a duty to answer their government's call to arms.

She'd thought that Louise had taken her granda's death and the subsequent move in her stride, poor lamb. She'd loved the farm and cried for hours at the thought of leaving it behind, but the prospect of living close enough to Leslie Mulligan to walk up the hill and visit, instead of waiting for Evelyn to drive her, had appeared to have lessened some of the hurt.

While Louise had sought comfort from her friend, sorting out the new place *had* given Evelyn something of her own to focus on in those early months. It had been quite the challenge, trying to make the room that had once served as the shopfront into a serviceable living area. She'd dusted off her sewing machine, and sewn curtains and furnishings for that and all of the rooms. After a time, she'd begun to enjoy the unconventionality of the building, and delighted in the quirky points of interest. The milkshake machine, left over from the shop days and stashed in the shed out the back, still worked, so she'd brought it inside and they'd developed a routine of making luscious milk-bar-style thickshakes in the kitchen for after-school treats. And the old cash register, made to accept only imperial money, had been salvaged from the back-room cupboard and since then had sat, cumbersome and clunky, on the solid timber counter running the length of what had become their lounge room, along with Louise's framed drawings and wonky pottery bowls from various school projects.

She's sitting on the couch in the dark, tossing up the merits of going to bed now, at 7.30 pm, and risking being awake for the day before 3.00 am, when she's disturbed by a sharp rapping at the door. Startled, she pulls her threadbare chenille dressing-gown around her and moves towards it, reaching for the axe handle she keeps close by – not that she seriously expects that she'd be any match for anyone. She hasn't told Louise that since a month or two back, when a number of bodies were found stuffed into barrels in an old bank vault in a dying town much like this one, she's taken to sleeping with a knife under her pillow and an axe handle by the door. Louise'd worry about her, of course, if she ever revealed her secret. But she'd laugh and cover up her concern for her silly old gran, and point out that South Australia and Snowtown were a damn long way from here. The murders had really shaken her, though. It was a rude awakening to realise just how old and vulnerable she might appear – and be – stuck here, halfway up the hill, with nobody within cooee. Until that news story broke, she'd never really been fearful of being on her own.

The person on the other side of the door coughs, a manly clearing of the throat, and raps again.

'You there, Mrs…Evelyn? It's me, Leslie.'

Hiding the axe handle behind the ludicrously extravagant floral umbrella Louise bought for her the last time she visited her, she smooths her hands over her dressing-gown, pats her hair down, unhooks the chain, and opens the door.

'Leslie. Come in.'

She opens the door widely and waves him in, asking him to excuse her appearance. 'Just had a lovely long soak in the bath. Come on through. Family not with you?' She peers behind him, trying to see into the car.

'Nah. They're with Mum,' he says, wiping his feet and entering the house. 'They're all pretty shattered after the day on the road. Just thought I'd swing by before it got too late and say g'day properly.'

Leading him to the lounge room, Evelyn indicates that he should sit down.

'I'll go pop the kettle back on. Just boiled a few minutes ago. Got some Anzacs somewhere, from the CWA fundraiser. Not my own, I'm afraid.'

Leslie's sitting opposite her, empty teacup and plate in front of him, his wallet pulled out, and half a dozen tatty photos spread between them.

He laughs. 'Well, one wife is an ex now and she's found herself a new pot of gold. And the first three kids, they're practically grown. They come and go between us as they please. So it's not as mad as it seems. Starting to take holidays now and then, too. Went to Italy and saw Sil's parents' homeland with them when Lenny was just a coupla months old.'

He picks up one of the photos and shows Evelyn. 'This one here? Clara, the eldest. She's going to take over from me one day soon, I reckon. She doesn't look like much, tiny little scrap that she is, but she's got all the blokes quaking in their boots.'

Evelyn reaches for the photo and, picking up the glasses from the chain around her neck, slides them back over her nose and examines the photo, turning it this way and that.

'She's very like you.'

'Yep, born about a year after I shot through to work on my uncle's boat. Unexpected. Dumb teenage stuff. Married her mother and, silly buggers we were, went and had two more kids. Took us a decade to figure out what a stupid pair of clowns we'd been.'

Evelyn moves the photo close and then away from her face. She'd like to go and get her magnifying glass from the kitchen drawer, but Leslie might think it odd if she were to take an excessive interest in the young woman.

It's the eyes that interest her. She'd always noticed them first and they'd remain imprinted in her mind for a long time afterwards. She'd never forgotten that first look into each of her own babies' eyes. Olive'd had steely blue-grey eyes with the tiniest fleck of brown gazing foggily into hers. She knew then, seeing that fleck, that one day she'd have her father's eyes. And little Petey, his were a mystery. When he grew up, she'd thought at the time, he'd be a surprise package. Louise had been six months old before Evelyn had gazed into her eyes and wondered what life held in store for her. And the other baby, well, she'd refused to look. Much to her regret, now. It would've been nice to have one memory, at least.

She leans forward and picks up a photo of Lenny kissing his newborn baby sister and re-examines it. He looks nothing like her Len, of course.

'You aren't offended?'

'By you naming him after Len? Don't be silly. I'm pleased that you can remember him fondly, and not…'

'He was good to me. Forever finding excuses to take me'n Loulie into town for ice-cream or a swim at the pool.'

'Via the front bar, of course,' Evelyn says. 'He always was a conniving old bugger.'

It'd taken years for her to be able to think back on those memories without feeling a flash of rage. She'd worn herself out over the years, fighting her emotions, denying that she was furious at what Len had done to them. But she's mellowed with time. For it *was* a sickness that made her husband behave in that way, even if they didn't recognise it then.

'Yes, sneaky, but to us kids sometimes he was a lot of fun.'

Leaning forward to pat Leslie's forearm, Evelyn agrees. Len could indeed be a lot of fun. No point telling Leslie about the flipside, and perhaps he was acknowledging that, anyway, by saying *sometimes*.

'I can only imagine how hard it was for you, and your whole family, when your dad disappeared like that.'

'Yeah, it was…Trying to convince Mum to come and live in Geraldton with us,' he says. 'She's finally been forced to accept that the old man won't be back. Don't like our chances of getting her to agree to come, though, I'm afraid.'

'Did I ever tell you that Louise thought she saw your dad in Dublin?' Evelyn starts.

'Dublin? Why would she have thought that?'

Evelyn pauses. Why did she raise *that*? She's always unsure about the divide between what she can and cannot say, when it comes to her granddaughter. She'd told her once about Leslie visiting her a few years earlier, and Louise had clammed right up, telling her grandmother to remember what she'd told Louise while growing up. *Our business is our business.* She didn't want Leslie, or anyone, knowing the ins and outs of her private life, and, equally as important, she didn't want to know anything about his or anyone else's. Occasionally, Evelyn'd slip. So happy to see Louise after such a long time that things she'd meant to keep inside would slide out. But mostly she managed to restrain herself.

She decides that now that she's started, she'll keep going.

'Just after she arrived in Dublin,' she tells him, 'she was running to jump on a train, and she thought she saw him. She said it couldn't have been more than a moment or two. He was built like your dad. Had thick, dark hair, and wore a striped blood-spattered butcher's apron. By the time Louise had composed herself, she'd remembered how since he'd started balding prematurely, everyone in town had called your dad *Eagle*.'

Leslie sits, stoic, and after she stops talking, Evelyn feels clumsy and old, and insensitive, too.

It had been late one night, on Evelyn's last trip, when Louise had told her about seeing that man. It was the same night – and the first time since her grandfather's death, as far as Evelyn can remember – that Louise'd spoken to her of Len, in a roundabout way, at least. Her granddaughter had recalled her longing to be part of the Mulligan family, and of how she'd felt gutted, betrayed even, by Eagle Mulligan leaving his family like that. Among the family, in their overcrowded corrugated-iron and timber worker's cottage, she'd always felt included, and participated in the boisterous games the children played with their father. She'd told Evelyn of how, after spending time at the Mulligans', she'd sometimes wonder if her father had muscly arms like Eagle Mulligan's – and if her grandfather, before he grew frail and sick, had been a strong man, too. Hearing that, even all those years later, had hit Evelyn hard.

'Dad died,' Leslie says after a few moments pass. 'Last year. I found out where he was a few years back and went to find him. He was already dead. Just a few months before I rocked up.' He sits quietly for a while. 'Turns out he lived in a fringe camp on the edge of a town in South Australia. Left a wife and six kids who relied on him to exist day to day like that. Dunno what happened. Can't have been just the meatworks shutting down, surely? Reckon the older I get, the less I understand about what makes people tick.'

Evelyn flinches, wondering if he has come for more than simply a casual visit.

He stands and moves over to the long bench running three-quarters the length of the room, and looks at the photographs.

'No recent ones?'

'No. I don't think Louise has let me take a photo of her since… well, since her grandad.'

He picks up a black-and-white photo of Olive, holding six-month-old baby Louise on her hip. It's Evelyn's only photo of the two of them together. Olive looks straight into the camera, unsmiling, perhaps already planning to leave her baby and run, unable to cope with being back with her parents after only several days. Louise looks like a stern little old man with the worries of the world on his shoulders. Where was *she* that day? She doesn't remember Len taking the photograph. Recalls only the sense of foreboding she'd felt when their daughter turned up on the doorstep after several years away – older, harsher, and more angry than she'd been, if that were possible, when she'd run away from home, stealing all Evelyn's jewellery – and her special dress, as she'd only discovered a couple of years later. *Don't call me Olive*, she'd demanded, walking straight in and plonking the scrappy baby in Evelyn's arms. *My name's Natalie now, and this is Elvira-Louise, your granddaughter.*

'Her mum was a looker in her day,' he says. 'Shame she never came back to see Louise. After Len died, I mean. Maybe…'

'Yes, she was,' she says, after a long pause. 'She died, too.' She's surprised at how raw the wound still feels when spoken aloud. 'Just under two years ago. I hadn't seen or heard from her for ages. Then one day, the day of Diana's funeral, I was at the shop, watching the service, and just as the little prince saluted his mother, young Constable Peterson walked in. No different to any other day; he could have been coming for Winfield Reds or chocolate milk. But as soon as I saw him, I knew.'

'I'm sorry…'

'No. No, it was a relief, actually, in a way. She was so very unhappy. They said it was that horrible disease that got her in the end. Not the drugs, not directly, anyway.'

In some respects, the hardest part of it all had been breaking it to Louise, all the way on the other side of the world. In the end, she'd called her at work, staying up until the middle hours of the night to be sure to catch her. *It's just us now,* Louise had said. *Us and somewhere...* The phone had cut out then. And when she'd tried to call the hotel back throughout the night, the phone had rung out each time.

'There was a lot of dumping and leaving going on in this town,' Leslie says, wryly. 'Reckon there must've been something in the drinking water.'

Evelyn tenses, half expecting a question. But if he is aware of the extent of the secrets she holds, he isn't letting on.

'I should go,' he adds a few moments later, replacing a school photo of Louise, aged thirteen, on the counter. 'Sil'll be wondering where I am.'

Evelyn stands, pulls her dressing-gown around her and leads the way to the front door. She pauses before unclipping the safety chain and twisting the deadlock.

'I hope I get to meet little Lenny before you go back,' she says. She can feel the unsaid words pushing their way through, but closes her mouth firmly to prevent their escape. Nothing to be gained now from upsetting more lives. 'Give my love to your mum.'

2005

Rendezvous

The return ferry has just left. She wishes she were on it, headed back to her rooming house. Back, even, to the grind at the perhaps ironically named Lucky Shamrock. The woman hands the paper cup across the counter, 'One Proper Coffee,' and turns back to the American soap opera on the television hung above the counter.

According to the sign, the Pumpkin Cafe specialises in *Proper Hot Coffee in a Paper Cup. Freshly baked cakes. Sarnies. Chilled drinks. Beer. Hot snacks.* A couple of minutes earlier, Louise had asked the woman behind the counter if she served chilled wine, a bit of Dutch courage. The woman looked her up and down and pointed to the sign. *Only beer. Chilled drinks are fizzy.*

Back at the table, she flicks through the newspaper, annoyed at herself for leaving her book on the ferry. She thinks about Gran sending away to the city for it after hearing the author speak on the radio. Imagines her receiving it some weeks later, pondering just the right words to write in the inside cover. Then lining up at the post office, shaking her head in disbelief at the cost of sending a book to Dublin from a little country town in Western Australia. She'd have considered hand delivering it, saving it until she took her trip in six months' time. Then sent it anyway.

As soon as Louise had realised her book was missing, she'd rushed back and asked to be allowed to go on board and retrieve it from her seat. Not finding it there, she'd tried to hide her upset as the cleaner scouted other areas of the ferry, and checked the lost property for her. She wonders what the mystery book thief will make of the strange inscription, a personal message intended for her eyes only. *I heard this young woman on the radio, I think that perhaps you'll relate to her.*

She looks out the window at the road in to the ferry port. He'd said he may be a little late. Teased her for being old-fashioned and quaint, for not having a cellular so he could contact her. Shook his head and pointed at his chest when she asked why on earth she would want to carry a phone around. *So you can speak with me, of course.*

Tilting her head, she brings the cup closer to her eyes and reads the fine print running down the side seam. *Caution: contents hot.* Sipping the coffee, she grimaces. The coffee *is* hot, but despite the bold claims on the cafe's signage, the paper cup seems to lack actual coffee.

She doesn't normally reveal anything of herself to guests. But he'd been coming to the hotel regularly for a while, greeting her with *Goodday, Kangaroo Mate*, and a grin. At breakfast, he'd ask questions while she refilled his coffee, paused his chewing, looked her in the eye as she answered. Little by little, she revealed snippets, redacted information. She'd left Australia years ago – alone. Was still alone. She'd got stuck in London for a bit, five years in total. She'd gone up to Scotland. Came here. Seemed to have stayed. Liked to read. Kept to herself. Was yet to visit Spain, his home country. She began to invent reasons and excuses to bump into him and make small talk. She learned that he was separated. No children. Own business. Ageing parents. Travelled a lot for work. Not as exciting as it sounded, he said. He'd been to Australia, once. Seen the Opera

House. Held a koala bear. She'd tried to set him straight. Attempted to use the riddle – How much can a koala bear? – but it fell flat. He didn't get it and it was too hard to explain in words that made sense to him. She was in his room then, closing his curtains, turning his bedclothes down, even though they didn't actually do that in the budget hotel. He'd looked at her. *You're strange...he'd* said, shaking his head...*I can't work you out.* As she turned to leave the room, he'd reached for her hand and raised it to his lips. Back home, she'd have said he was sleazy.

Until he checked in that morning two weeks back, she'd thought she'd been about to hand in her notice. As he signed the guest register, he'd asked her what was wrong. She hadn't realised she'd been displaying her emotions. She told him that she was reading a book that made her sad, and homesick. She missed the sun and space. Asked him if he'd ever heard of a lawn made of mint. There was one in the book, she said. And she could almost smell it. She'd started to cry then. Said she was sick of the bloody endless rain and grey skies, of the moaning voices and miserable faces, of pretty green lawns that were too soggy to sit on. She was the only Australian in a tiny Irish hotel staffed by Eastern Europeans who spoke basic, customer-service-level English – and there was barely an Irish person to be found here. She said she was lonely, and wanted real conversation. That she worked like a bloody dog, for less than peanuts. She stopped herself then. *Oops. Sorry.* She grinned. *Welcome to the Lucky Shamrock.* She handed him his key.

You need some fun, he'd said.

When he'd gone up to his room, she locked the front door of the hotel and turned the *Back in 5 mins* sign to face outside. Out the back, puffing on her cigarette, she'd thought of Gran on her last visit, urging her to at least try and find a better job, if she was still intent on not coming home. *Stubborn to the end...*And she knew then that one day, but not just yet, she would return home.

She forced Gran out of her mind and thought about the Australian sky. She ached for it lately, mourned its absence along with all the other absences. She wished sometimes that she could paint, so she could try and capture it, and keep it on her wall. She'd once had a two-week thing with an English painter, for no other reason than he'd told her that he'd visited the outback and painted landscapes when he was a student. He named the colours he'd used to try and do the sky justice – ultramarine, cerulean, cobalt, steel, turquoise, peacock, vermillion, violet, sapphire. As he described it, she'd thought of all those blues stretching to the horizons – luscious rich red in the north, bleached straw in the middle, and, in the south, deep blue-green so you couldn't tell if it was trees or ocean meeting the eggshell blue horizon.

She'd stubbed out her cigarette and gone up to Raimond's room on the pretext of checking for clean towels. Her heart thumped in her chest and her hands sweated. *What kind of fun?* she'd asked. He suggested she meet him somewhere on her next weekend off. She indulged in a fantasy for just a moment or two – of packing a suitcase, getting rid of anything that wouldn't fit, of leaving Dublin and heading somewhere else, his somewhere else. She truly could start afresh – reinvent herself – maybe even learn his language so that his ageing parents were utterly charmed by her efforts. *Take a risk. What are you afraid of?* Raimond had teased as she backed out of the room carrying two perfectly clean bundled-up towels. *I will bring more towels in five minutes,* she'd called, a little too loudly, from the hallway.

Back at the room with his replacement towels, she'd said that she wasn't afraid of the likes of him. And that yes, she *would* spend her next weekend off with him. She wanted to have some fun. For close to two years, she'd been in the same temporary job. Shifting between the reception desk, scrubbing toilets, serving breakfast and making beds for hotel guests who'd treated her at best as a servant and at worst as something unsavoury that they'd dragged in off the footpath on the bottom of their sensible walking shoes.

All that she had to do, he'd told her before checking out a day later, was take the ferry across when she finished work on Friday week, and he'd meet her in the cafe on the dock. *No stringing attached.* She laughed at that. Didn't bother explaining. He had a meeting scheduled that day with clients in the town. He could stay for the weekend. Fly home on Monday after putting her on the ferry back to Dublin. He'd peeked at the staff roster hanging by the counter. Knew she'd be back in time for her afternoon shift. She'd asked him, *Are you some kind of stalker?* He didn't answer. *It will be our first weekend rendezvous.* When he said that, she felt giddy.

A rendezvous sounded exciting, illicit. She can't recall the last time she'd felt so excited about anything. She doesn't dream big. Keeps herself plain. Doesn't seek adventure. If anything, it is anonymity she seeks. When not in her work uniform, she hides underneath oversized long-sleeved tops, windcheaters, Levi's 501s and Doc Martens. But as he said it, she'd imagined the thigh-high skirts and barely-there tops worn by the outrageously beautiful women in the James Bond VHS movies she'd occasionally watch in the evenings, sitting out on the verandah, when she'd lived in the Kimberley for a while. She'd intend to watch the movie but inevitably become distracted by the endless dark sky, lit up by more stars than she could begin to count. Gazing up at it, she'd wonder if she'd ever truly leave her past behind.

Raimond had looked perplexed as she laughed at his invitation. Said he was being serious. She tried to make light of it. If she rendezvoused with him, she'd told him, she'd have to leave the Levi's at home and invest in something dangerous.

Now that she is waiting, looking out the window at what she assumes is the entire town spread before her, she thinks that she understands why he chose to meet her here, in this strange little port on the edge of northern Wales. Nobody is likely to see him out in public with a plain Australian, middle-aged and turned to flab, thanks to too much stodgy food.

She'd told only one of her workmates, Eliya, of her weekend plans, and even she, with her differing values to Louise's, had warned her not to go, said that it was unlikely that he considered her more than a distraction from the round of tedious monthly meetings with clients. Louise'd tried to sound jovial, saying she was only going for a bit of fun, and was satisfied with being a distraction. But Eliya had reminded her that Dublin is an hour or two from just about anywhere, and that, unlike Eliya, Louise had a valid passport. He could have met her in Dublin after his meeting and together they could have flown to Italy, France or Spain for the same price – and in less time than it would take the ferry to cross the Irish Sea.

Since leaving Australia, duds are the only men she's allowed to get close to her. The one rule she imposes on herself is that she will not knowingly get involved with a partnered man. She asks the same question of each of the duds, aware of the fact that without insisting they sign a statutory declaration, she has only their word that they are single. She quietly prides herself on this being a significant point of difference between her and Eliya, a woman she sometimes struggles not to judge harshly. There have been a string of lonely losers with broken hearts out for a short rebound fling. Australian travellers claiming not to have girlfriends or wives back home, various one-night stands, just so she could hear the accent for a while. The occasional workmate – a cook, dish pig or bartender in this or that dingy hotel or pub. Unreliable, unhygienic – and only two steps ahead of the law, some of them. Rarely anyone she was actually drawn to. Never what her gran might call a *prospect*.

Two and a half hours' rolling around the rough waters of the sea lane, trying to hold the contents of her stomach in and hoping that the drunken Irish football team on their end-of-season jaunt would do likewise, followed by almost an hour of waiting – stood up, probably – in this odd little cafe, and she's thinking that she should have listened to Eliya.

In the corner of the cafe, a pale, skinny boy with protruding teeth and a worried expression looks like he's about to give up on his dreams and leave the *Deal or No Deal* poker machine. For the past half-hour, she's watched him feed it, one coin at a time. About fifteen minutes in, she'd decided that if he gave up without winning something, she'd change her ticket and take the next ferry back to

Dublin. She might sit here all weekend, otherwise, looking more pathetic by the hour.

A girl of around the same age as the boy enters the cafe, wearing a faded, once-red tracksuit and sports shoes. Passing Louise, she walks straight to the boy and whispers something, before demanding loudly that he follow her. *Now!* She turns and walks back towards the cafe entrance and, slowing momentarily in front of Louise, meets her eye and smirks before continuing. Sometimes Louise privately envies women who exude as much confidence as this teenage girl, though she can't imagine herself actually desiring such control over anyone.

Once when she was about eleven, she'd stood in front of Leslie Mulligan, just before he had a growth spurt and towered over her. Pulling petals off a daisy one at a time, she'd stared him in the eyes. *He loves me. He loves me not.* Watched his face grow pinker by the second. *He loves me…*She'd run off laughing, aware that she'd developed some sort of mysterious power over him, but not yet knowing how or when to use it. Hid in her tree house for ages. Too embarrassed to come down. Peered through the gaps between the wooden planks and felt bad as Granda blasted him for not looking out for her. *What if she's in the dam, you dumb bastard?* Knowing full well his granddaughter was half fish but having to blame someone else for his inattention. But she didn't come down until Leslie'd gone home.

The boy pats his pockets as the last coin drops. He turns to see if the girl is still outside, and walks quickly past Louise towards her.

Louise'll give Raimond ten more minutes. The next ferry's not due for ages, anyway.

Before he'd finished checking out the last time and she'd confirmed that she really would come, they'd studied the timetable and agreed which ferry she'd take. After signing his bill, he'd grinned. *We'll have fun*, he said, and walked towards the door.

She thinks of a funny story to tell Raimond. That strange meal she'd had before leaving Dublin. She's seen, and served, some odd stuff in her time abroad, usually wrapped in batter and deep-fried.

This one was different, show-offy. A potato – Greek style, according to the menu – a scooped-out jacket potato stuffed with baked beans from a can. Melted bright yellow processed cheese oozing all over the edges of the plate onto the white tablecloth. A 'salad' of wilted lettuce, and nothing else. Kalamata olive rings from a can on the side. She'd taken her camera out of her handbag and photographed the meal. The waiter – more Ukrainian, she suspected, than Greek – had looked at her, puzzled, and asked, *Why for you are taking photos of your luncheon?*

She'd answered, quick as a blink: *I'm a food writer...*Smiling up at him...*And this meal is bloody splendid.*

She knows that when she tells Raimond the story, some of the Australian-English nuances will be lost on him. That's partly why she'll tell him. She wonders if maybe she would make a good food writer. She'd read an article about a new trend online. People like to read blogs and forums written by everyday people. They want to connect with personal stories and experience, and don't want to read the opinions of pretentious experts. Perhaps she could take photos of her meals, upload them to the internet and write funny stories about them. Although you'd probably have to be missing a few brain cells to want to look at photos of other people's dinner.

She looks up as Raimond rushes in. 'Sorry, sorry.' She stands and hoists her jeans up, pulls the cuffs of her windcheater down so her wrists and hands are covered. She tries to do the continental air kiss thing. Clunks her teeth hard on his ear. Starts telling him about the soccer hooligans. Says she loves that word. Her Granda was always calling her a hooligan when she ran amok.

'Slow down. You are speaking too fast.' He takes a step back and smiles. 'You look...Nothing dangerous and new?'

She regrets for a moment that she hadn't gone shopping. But reminds herself she'd decided that if she intended to begin breaking her own rules, then she was going to do it on her own terms. 'Maybe next time,' she says. And asks him if he thinks she would make a good food writer.

2012

Dodgy narratives

I'm trying to work out how to make a storyline that sees Meredith, the beautiful, blonde (of course) thirty-five year old architect walk out of a very important client meeting in order to have a quickie in the print room with the twenty-two year old hot guy who delivers the toner for the office printers. Dirk's brief says that Meredith is a career woman, mother of two, and though she's prone to slipping out of work to meet various younger men for casual sex, she's madly in love with her partner of ten years. Dirk is insistent that I include these details. He believes that it will make it more relatable for the readership. Since the magazine did one of those readership surveys last year, he's constantly micromanaging my writing and throwing in extra detail to include. I pay my bills this way, so I write what I'm told to write. Seventy per cent of respondents to the survey came from the same demographic. Somehow I doubt that the majority of those readers, women of the British council estates, are going to relate to Meredith, at all.

Since Gran left last month, I've found it hard to get back into the swing of churning out these 'real-life' stories. She'd pointedly suggested that I aim higher, that if I must write real-life stories, I do so for quality magazines with thick, glossy covers. *Or even* the *Reader's Digest, for heaven's sake.* I don't know why she's grown disdainful of the *Reader's Digest.* After all, I learned to read by devouring Granda's old copies. I make a mental note to ask, next time we Skype, if she's signed up for an Introduction to Literature class since finishing her course in French History for Beginners at the community college classes at the district high school.

I didn't know, until she'd made those comments, that she'd seen the stories I write, or that the backwater newsagents in town would stock the cheap British imports. I felt embarrassed for her, imagining her going up to the counter with the magazine and its lurid headlines. 'My Precocious Neighbour. Afternoons with the Postman (he *always* rings twice).' I'd never told her the publications I wrote for, or my nom-de-plume. When pushed, she admitted that she'd emailed and asked Raimond for the details – and had the magazine ordered in specially – that is, until she realised how trite it was and cancelled the order. And though I have never met the latest newsagent in town, I burned with embarrassment at the thought of him knowing that Gran was less than impressed with my efforts.

She wanted to read a story with my own name on it, she'd said. An intelligent story, not one of the trashy romps credited to Crystal Dawn, or any one of the other ridiculous aliases I adopt for my work.

As if that weren't bad enough, that night, after Raimond arrived, she'd set about picking apart the inconsistencies in the story that she'd read on the plane after spotting the latest magazine at Heathrow while waiting for her flight across the Channel to see me. I'd been mortified at the thought of my gran sitting there in economy class with *Real Confessions* open, tut-tutting at my clumsy attempts at what really amounted to little more than soft lady porn presented within a flimsy narrative arc. I tried to speak up for what I do, attempted to make it sound harder than it really is to write material that is suggestive but does not push into territory that would require the magazine to be wrapped in plastic before being sold to the general public. She tutted some more and said, *Darling, it's certainly not Anaïs Nin.* Raimond put his hand over his mouth and stared intently at his stupid spreadsheets, his shoulders shuddering as he attempted to suppress his mirth. I lost it at both of them then.

I don't believe for one second that Meredith, or any of the other caricatures that turn up in my inbox each week as a series of dot points to be included in my stories, exist outside Dirk's perverted mind. In the brief period I knew him in that way, Dirk had a pretty twisted imagination. He used to get off on me turning up at his room, grotty from hours of cleaning work, wearing my work clothes and carrying a duster in my hand. The way he'd respond when he opened the door to my quiet knocking, you'd have thought I'd dressed up for the occasion. I can easily imagine him sitting there, jotting down the bullet points of his puerile fantasies and sending them to me to flesh out. Though he swears on his new trophy wife's life (not his own, I notice) that the stories are true, I sometimes wonder what sort of woman would take time out of her life to email her secret confessions to a dodgy male editor in the hope of having them brought to life by a hack writer in his cheap magazine.

'Who even reads these shitty magazines nowadays?' I say it out loud, as though I expect Raimond to answer me, but I'm ruminating, really.

'Remember I told you I was writing a novel? What happened?' I *am* speaking to him now. And I'm aware that I sound like I'm fifteen.

A few days after Gran returned to Australia, Raimond suggested that I'd never developed emotionally past that age. He'd been talking with Gran, he said, and he wondered what had happened at that stage in my life. He ran his hands over my neck as he spoke, wrapped the hair that was too short to pull into my ponytail into curls around his fingers. In the beginning, I was so starved for touch that I'd practically purr when he did that. But that day I'd wondered if he knew that he was pulling the hairs roughly at the nape of my neck. *Was it something to do with your mother?* I'd said nothing.

He's become something of an amateur therapist since his *American ex-wife*, as he calls Tilda, has been seeing a psychologist and reporting back to him. When he got off the phone to her that afternoon he raised it, he told me that the psychologist suspected that something in Tilda's emotional journey had caused her to *cease maturation* beyond a certain age. He'd reported that she'd had ten sessions attempting to get to the cause of it and they were still none the wiser.

Ten sessions, to work out nothing? What a rort. I wanted to be mature and not question the level of intimacy he still shares with someone he refers to as a witch behind her back. In his role as amateur therapist, he'd told me that he felt that Tilda had matured to her early twenties – the time she'd met him, oddly enough – whereas in his opinion, I had only made it as far as fifteen. Though he'd technically split with her, it was clear that, in his view, Tilda was still something to be solved. Still one of his problems. I was furious at the thought he'd never let her go and walked out of the room, quietly singing *How do you solve a problem like Tilda?* Pretty much just as a fifteen-year-old girl might, I suppose.

Raimond grunts something indecipherable without looking up from the spreadsheets and invoices spread over my kitchen table. He is not proud of my work. I don't know what he tells people about what I do for a living. If he tells people anything at all, for that matter. Perhaps, when we are apart, I am nothing more than an absence – a space, or a question mark – in all of the thoughts and the conversations he holds. But, given that I can earn as much from banging out one crap story in a couple of hours as I used to from cleaning toilets and stripping beds for a full week, he'd kept quiet when I revealed my plans to do that temporarily, just until I sold my first novel.

When the email from Dirk came out of the blue, he'd acted as though he was jealous. In fairness to Raimond, I *had* allowed him to think that there was more to Dirk and me than there had been. I'd neglected to mention, for as long as I thought that I could get away with it, that I finished knocking on Dirk's door after spending a third weekend with Raimond in that grotty little town, a ferry ride and a country away. In his email, Dirk had said he liked me, despite my having dumped him like that. He'd admired the way, he'd said, that I'd put myself through night school. Then his offer – perhaps I would like some work writing for the magazine he'd just taken over as editor? He completely overstated the literary qualities of the publication, and, flattered to have been commissioned without even trying, I signed the contract. While it was hardly the writing work of my dreams, I reasoned that it would free me up to spend more time on my novel, and that I could move here, to this Spanish village. And that when Raimond visited, on those rare occasions when we left the bedroom and went out to eat, I wouldn't stink of bleach and toilet freshener. Although I wasn't ready then to say it out loud, I dared to imagine that there might be a future for us.

'What I mean is, what sort of person would walk into the back of a newsagency on some grotty council estate and seek out these tacky covers when they could go home and search the internet for something equally badly written for no outlay?'

He used to find my outbursts amusing. Or he said he did, anyway. But now, he starts going on about how, despite being well into the new millennium, many homes in England are not yet connected to the internet. I'm pretty certain he pulls these facts out of his arse, for I never see evidence of any of his claims. Then he says what he really thinks.

'I suspect the women of the house don't want to be seen to be reading that dubious material online. It is easier to hide a crappy magazine than an internet search – for the technologically challenged.'

That stings. I decide that maybe Meredith doesn't love her life so much, after all, and perhaps her husband has some sort of perversion that goes way beyond a preference for her to be blindfolded and dressed in a taffeta skirt. Perhaps he's an arrogant and opinionated European with commitment issues.

Raimond says that I don't know poverty, that I have led a privileged life and should not judge others.

'You are defending the women who buy it? But judge me?'

Whatever he thinks of the stories, they are still my work. Before I leave the room and go outside, I remind him that when we'd met I was a maid in a two-star hotel, scrubbing other people's shit out of toilet bowls for a living. Not a good deal of privilege there, but I took a level of pride in making sure there were no disgusting drag stripes left in the bowl.

The morning before he'd arrived, unannounced, when Gran was last here, I'd told her that I thought that maybe, finally, I was able to commit to a future with him.

Has he got around to that divorce yet? She used her special voice, the one that sounds innocuous but is actually loaded with subtext. If it hadn't become glaringly obvious since her last visit that she is growing increasingly frail, perhaps I'd have retaliated. Or at least defended myself. On a roll by then, she said that she was going to speak her mind once and for all, because she was old and I was dense, and she'd been excusing both my stupidity and my bad decisions since I was a child. I should come home, she'd said, where I belong. I could have the house, do it up, run a business in the front rooms... *Write as much smut as you want.*

That evening, having turned up claiming that he'd had to cancel his meetings in Dublin, Raimond sat himself down at the head of the table like the King, spread his papers out in front of him and observed as Gran and I – or mostly I – had polished off a bottle of red wine. I was touchy with Gran. She was right. This whole situation really was going nowhere. Maybe it finally was time to go back to where I'd come from. At nearly fifty, I had very little to show for my life.

Gran had raised the issue of his divorce, or non-divorce, then. I sat – at first seething, then humiliated – while he told us some cock-and-bull story about his sensitive ex-wife. She was still seeing a psychologist. Still couldn't be without him. Still every other cliché in the still-married man's handbook. I'd seen her on television the week before, and had smuggled her self-indulgent piece of crap book into the house and read it while he was away. How could he defend her, the now-famous American writer, travelling the country and speaking of her memoir of her amusingly clichéd and tormented life with a successful and self-defined handsome Spanish businessman?

Eventually he comes outside to find me. I'm sitting on the back steps, watching the sky change colour as dusk approaches.

'It's never going to be right,' I say.

I've tried on and off over the years to try and explain the sadness and loneliness, the isolation that I feel when I look up and see the slightly skew-whiff shades of blue and grey of the northern hemisphere.

Once I begged him to come with me, just for a visit, to see my part of Australia, and the sky. I felt that I needed to see if I could be brave enough to go back – to go home – to face my past. He'd refused. He was still officially living with Tilda then. He could break away, he'd said, for days to see me. But he could never leave her for too long. She was unstable, and he'd never be able to live with himself if she did something erratic.

I know, as he sits next to me and takes my hand in his, that he is aware that I am not referring just to the wrongness of the colours in the sky.

It is too late but I ask him again now. 'Just a short trip?'

'There is nothing of interest for me there,' he says.

And in that moment I know that if there was ever someone I *could* have made a future with, it was not him.

But I refuse to concede. 'I wish I'd met you before you met her.'

Can I sound more desperate? I backtrack and say that I'd like to have met him before he became a damaged man who was still deeply in love with the *idea* of his American ex-wife. And that, in that ideal world, I'd have come without a trailer load of baggage, too. I can't seem to stop.

I add that I had thought for a long time that maybe he was the love of my life; the one I had been waiting for; the one I'd let my guard down for, and let in – all of that. I laugh and say that it seems I have turned us into a Nick Cave ballad somewhere along the way. But really, though, we've become a rather lonely and strange habit.

'Your grandmother is right,' he says. 'You should go home.'

I'm crying now. Not the great melodramatic sobs that usually accompany our arguments. Rather, it's a purging. Finally, an acceptance that whatever it was we had, or I thought we had, has truly and completely run its course.

It is growing dark. I use my index finger and write the word *Fin* in large loopy letters in the air in front of us. He's right, of course. I won't pretend to be offended. I'm done. I lean in to him and rest my head on his shoulder.

2013

Leaving Elvis

I walk in the door and Gran tells me that a month ago, Leslie Mulligan was taken by a shark while trying to save a stranger. Imagine, a national hero. She actually says that. As though dying in a world of pain in an ocean filled with his own blood was a heroic choice.

Awake for thirty hours, I'm beyond tired and probably in shock. I thought about Leslie Mulligan for much of the flight home, only managing to relax a little after deciding to look him up, get it out of my system once and for all. I'd planned what to say. I'd be nonchalant and keep it simple. I'd shake his hand and say, *Hello. A lot of water under the bridge, eh*? Perhaps, if it went well, in time I could reveal more.

To mask any awkwardness, I ask Gran when they're erecting the statue in his memory. Maybe because I am jetlagged and crazy with exhaustion, I laugh when she tells me that it is already being discussed. She insists on turning on her computer and bringing up the town website with all the proposals that have come in so far. There's to be a vote at next month's council meeting. The most preposterous design, hand-sketched, depicts him wrestling a shark. The poor creature is held in a headlock and Leslie, looking strangely like Norm from those *Life. Be in it* ads from the seventies, grins victoriously. The local artist, a Year 12 student named Russell, has apparently forgotten that the shark won that particular battle.

As is her habit, Gran tells me that each time Leslie came home to visit, first alone and then with wife number two and their children, he'd asked after me. As is mine, I wonder if she ever believed my story, but don't ask. She reminds me that she'd always talked me up; telling him, for example, that when I worked as a maid in a dotty little hotel in Dublin, I managed the hotel. More recently, she'd claimed that I was a serious writer for important European magazines. She'd first told me this while visiting me last year, before Raimond – the one I'd kidded myself was *the one* – left to resume life in the next village with the wife I had understood to be living on another continent. *You would not believe the life I have you lead,* she'd chortled, hugging me close to her chest while I sobbed and wondered why, after so many years, she still felt she had to lie about me. It was painfully obvious to me, then, how frail she had grown. Previously warm and comforting, that day she'd felt cold, angular, sharp-edged. Gran was a shrunken woman.

She played on that new frailty when, within weeks of her return to Australia, she summoned me from overseas – more urgently than she ever had in the past. She said that for all these years, she'd been traipsing around the less savoury parts of Australia and the wider world to see me, and now it was time for me to come home. She wanted to go out with a bit of dignity intact, in her own home, surrounded by her only family.

We moved into this house, about a kilometre from the centre of town, at the start of my second year of high school. It was strange, at first, being off the farm. Though we had been only five kilometres out of town, it was a different life for us both. Home was now a weird little part-shop/part-house that had once been a petrol station and general store. In place of paddocks and a vast garden, we had cracked bitumen and rotting wooden boards covering up the holes where they'd removed the bowsers. For a while, Gran had tried to make it nice, planting a garden in pots, but she lost interest pretty quickly and everything soon died.

One good thing about living halfway up the hill like that was being able to see all the comings and goings. I entertained myself by making up stories about the exploits of the locals. Not that there was much activity in a quiet town on the edge of nowhere. Once a forest, there were few large trees left between our new house and the cemetery in the centre of town. The settlers like my great-grandfather, who had come to re-establish lives in the bush after the war, saw to that. They'd stopped fighting in other countries, only to come here and start chopping down trees. Gran's theory was that they'd got so used to being in the trenches and bayoneting other men, they needed to keep on killing in order to feel normal.

When she first began trying to coerce me into coming back, Gran told me that the district was becoming increasingly fashionable with tree-changers. *There are quirky little 'retro' shops and bed-and-breakfasts spreading throughout the district.* Maybe she'd forgotten that during my first years away, she'd written letters filled with ideas like opening a place to sell milkshakes and souvenirs to tourists once the sale of the farm was sorted out. She'd eventually bought the old converted petrol station she'd rented since we'd left the farm together, but I suspect much of the extra money was spent on her annual visits to see me, wherever in the world I was, around the time of my birthday. *The old fifties shop fittings are probably worth a small fortune on eBay,* she'd said in one of her emails some years later. *Vintage is in vogue,* she'd reminded me again, just a few months ago, via one of our Skype calls. *Maybe you could do the place up, set yourself up for the future.* Then, not convinced I was listening, she'd resorted to pleading. *Come home.* By then I'd booked my ticket back.

By the middle of my second year of high school, Gran wanted me to stop spending so much time alone in the house with Leslie.

She said it was not his fault, that he was older than me and I was *developing*. I thought this was unfair. Leslie had always been welcome before, and Gran had said many times that he'd saved me from myself when everything happened with Granda. But Gran was still prone to outpourings of rage and grief, and I didn't want to antagonise her. Whenever we went back to my place after school, I would look out for Gran at the end of her shift. When I saw her car pass the cemetery turn-off, I'd shove Leslie out the back door and we'd run through the scrub to the path that met up with the road around the bend. Each time I forced him out the back door like that, I apologised. I hoped he believed that Gran was just miserable about the job she had been doing to support us now that we had moved off the farm.

She'd cried every night after starting that job. People weren't even treated like real people anymore, she'd said. They sat in the dining area, some tied to chairs, drooling and decaying while she moved around, spoonfeeding the top lip and scraping the excess from the bottom, just like they were babies.

She continued to worry all that year about the problem of my ever-growing breasts. Maybe it was while tending to the elderly that she came up with her solutions. *You must never be in a bedroom alone with a boy. Keep yourself nice. Always remain clothed.* I repeatedly broke rule number one. But in all that time alone in my bedroom, the closest Leslie and I came to breaking the others was asking Elvis about his state of dress or undress in the bathroom on the day he died.

We were at Leslie's place, out of town and further up the hill, the day things changed, the day I stopped keeping myself nice and stripped myself down to a semi-clothed state. His bedroom was out the back, an old curvy-bodied 1950s caravan that someone had donated to the family when child number five or six came along. With the van plonked between the outside dunny and the sleepout for his younger brothers, it was like having his own flat, he told me. The rest of the family were out that day, and it was unusually quiet without a stream of Leslie's siblings pouring in and out of the small caravan and bothering us. I pretended that this is what it would be like if I was married or had a real boyfriend instead of just reliable old brotherly Leslie.

While he sat on the caravan step, I lay across his narrow bed, half-heartedly trying to finish *The Unauthorised (but True) Biography of Elvis Presley*. I gave a running commentary – tried to involve him. Was Elvis buried in a gilded tomb like Tutankhamun? What did he think Lisa Marie had placed there for her dad to take into the afterlife?

After a while, Leslie came into the van. I put the book on the floor and told him we'd have to ask Elvis. I said we should go to Graceland, just the two of us, as soon as we were both done with school. He sat on the end of the bed and started getting weird. He said there were other things than Elvis Presley, that he had been going along with all this stuff since *you know what* and it was time to move on. He started talking about how, when he was out by the river, when there was nobody else around, he felt at one with the universe. He said that standing on the riverbank, waiting for a fish to bite, he would feel the hairs on the back of his neck rise and wonder if it was because he was doing what he loved most, fishing. He added that after a good catch, he experienced what he thought must be true happiness. He felt strong, too – like a man.

I snorted, rolled about on the skinny little bed, holding my stomach, tears soaking my cheeks, not knowing if I was laughing or crying. Then he was on the bed straddling me, tickling my ribs. His face was red and he didn't look me in the eyes. I knew what that meant. I'd been hurting his feelings since we were kids. I used to – quite perversely – enjoy making him cry. But despite what he'd just said to me, I wanted him to feel happy, wanted him to feel strong, wanted him to feel like the man he'd felt like when he was out fishing. Just like he'd been when I cried all the time after Granda died, two days before Elvis.

He kept tickling me. I hated myself so much that I wanted to cry, but I faked laughter. Not knowing what to say, I reached up and kissed his mouth. Our teeth banged and his nose poked my eye and made it water, but we soon worked it out. Pulling his hand off my ribs, I shoved it up under my school dress and rubbed it back and forth outside of my knickers.

    I didn't know how much it would take to make things right again. So I just let him keep going. I stared at the tin roof and bit my lip while he inched my knickers down around my knees and thrashed about on top of me, making weird sounds like he was going to be sick all over my face. Before then I'd imagined that when I had proper sex it would hurt. But there was nothing, really, just his weight squashing the breath out of me and a mix of warmth and a dull scrapy tugging at my insides. Afterwards, I was embarrassed because I didn't bleed everywhere like I thought I should have. I lay there for a bit, not knowing what to say or feel. Noticing it was getting dark, careful to keep my eyes averted, I tidied myself up, repacked my schoolbag and left him lying there, staring at the roof, with a weird off-centre grin on his face.

Though smaller and shabbier than I recall, my old room is spotless, with new bedding and curtains, and a reading lamp on top of a pile of books. There are stickers on the spines of two of them. I must have neglected to return them to the library when, having served beer to enough locals to save an interstate fare, I fled. What if I were to return them now – *The Loneliness of the Long Distance Runner* and *I Never Promised You a Rose Garden* – bleakness and madness restored to their rightful place?

    I kneel on the floor beside my bed and, reaching beneath the metal frame with my right arm, sweep my fingertips across the lino. Extending them towards the wall, my shoulder pushes against the old bed frame. It isn't there. How strange that Gran should retain the books but not that. Then I remember disposing of the board after the last time I'd ever talked to Leslie Mulligan. Knowing we'd reached an impasse, I'd stormed off, and later traipsed back along the creek bed and dumped it among the wrecked fridges and decomposing animals, hoping that he would see it before he left, and decide to stay.

Exhausted as I am, I know I will not sleep until it is night-time in the northern hemisphere. I pad back to the lounge room and press the button on Gran's old computer. The computer is slow to boot up but fast enough for my techno-savvy gran to have stayed connected with me in recent years. I log on to my webmail. There is nothing from Raimond. I wasn't expecting anything. Not really. I email him, anyway. *I'm here, safe.* I don't sign it. I check my bank balance. If I am to be working from home and caring for Gran, I will need a new computer, a laptop, for privacy's sake. In recent years, stories written under various pseudonyms in *Real Confessions* and *Lonely Hearts* have been my bread and butter.

Inevitably, I revisit the website. Apparently, as well as being a national hero, Leslie Mulligan was a well-respected local boy. Though he left the town when he was seventeen, he came back regularly to visit his family for the first two decades – less frequently as his fishing fleet took him away for extended periods. The website also states that Leslie Mulligan had always planned to sell his fleet of fishing boats and come back to live in the town where he grew up. The story must have been invented by someone at the council. Gran told me several years ago that once his mother died, Leslie had never returned to the town.

Leslie avoided me at school for a few weeks, then stopped going altogether. One Sunday, after a few more weeks had passed, he came to see me when Gran was at work. Could we go for a walk down by the creek? We walked along, close but not touching, hands in our pockets, my eyes straight ahead. We reached the usual spot on the outskirts of town, beyond the old abattoir littered with car bodies and old fridges, and sat there, unspeaking, on the rotting vinyl car seats that had been put into the tray of an old ute. He was leaving, he said, going up north to work on the trawlers out of Geraldton.

I looked at an old bone sticking out of the brown sludge in the creek. Since we were little kids and I'd first started tagging along behind him, I'd believed they were animal bones from the old abattoir that popped out of the mud in different places along the creek's course.

Maybe they aren't animals, after all, I said to him that day. *Do you remember,* I'd asked, *how when I was little, Granda used to pay you to look after me when he was in town so he could drink at the RSL?*

Leslie said that he was sorry, but he didn't want to like me in that way and he was sorry for acting like he did. It was illegal, what he'd done; my gran would string him up for behaving that way. And my granda, well, he'd have killed him with his bare hands if he knew. He had to leave. We could be friends still – maybe – when he came back from fishing.

I said I was late, that I wouldn't tell Gran it was him. He wouldn't go to jail. *It can't be mine,* he said, *everybody knows it can't happen the first time.*

A week or so later, he waited for me outside the school gate. He wanted to talk. He said we could go north together, stay with his auntie. We could get special permission to be together. He'd asked around, and sometimes you could.

I said I had made a mistake and it wouldn't have been his, anyway. He seemed ready enough to accept this as true. His smile was the biggest I'd seen on him for a long time. I thought maybe if I wished for it hard enough, things would go back to how they were before. I asked him to come back and see if Elvis was about. I'd made new letters for the ouija board to commemorate the fact that it was nearly a year since his death, and said that I had a feeling that today Elvis might have a message for us from Granda. But he said he had things to do, that he was getting too old to be messing about, talking to ghosts. He said I should move on. Maybe he would see me another day. *We could still go north*, I said, but I was facing the back of his head. He was walking away, and I knew that we'd reached the ending.

Two days before I went into labour, I floated in the bath, observing from above my grossly distended form lolling in the bathtub. Water sloshed over the sides and soaked the bathmat. The bath was not large and my knees were bent up into the position the midwife told me I would use to deliver. My breasts were huge, blue vein tracks leading to nipples sitting atop like spotlights on a roo-shooter's four-wheel drive. I touched one nipple and was shocked to experience a tugging sensation right through to my distorted belly-button. I pinched my nipple tight and pulled hard, pretending to be a baby, sucking and stretching, trying to extract milk. I touched my stomach, hugged my huge gut and smiled at the face in the full-length mirror behind the door, serenely and smugly, like I had seen adult pregnant women do. Sinking lower into the water, I traced my fingers past the squiggling lump of baby and down between my legs. I hooked one leg over the bath edge and touched the hole where the baby would push through, circling slowly, then pressing hard against it. The throbbing ache in my stomach and groin had become so much a part of me that I had just about forgotten what it felt like not to be constantly aware of weight pushing against my body. Horrified, I discovered I could fit only three fingers halfway into my vagina. How would I stretch and avoid being slashed open? I screamed for my gran, who came rushing in to hoist me from the bath. She was strong enough to lift decaying old people from the bath, but not me. Clinging to my wet, naked body, she pulled me to her chest, rocking me back and forth and shooshing me. I was unable to cry, terrified that I would rip apart and that she would have to drag the pieces of me down to the end of the driveway to the car and take me away, down the hill and through town for everyone to see.

It has been nearly one year since Gran made what she deemed her final overseas trip to see me. She was glad, she'd said, that I had forced her to see three continents she'd never have seen otherwise. But she was done, too old to keep tootling off overseas. For the two months leading up to my return, Gran reminded me via Skype to 'ask the internet' about the goings-on in the political world. She was embarrassed, she said, possibly more times than she recalls, about what was going on. Earlier tonight, she reminded me that I must learn about the horseless men and the unspeakable things they are doing to the first woman other than the Queen ever to rule us.

Then she stunned me. In all those trips, we had never discussed them, those ghosts that accompanied me into every room, in every town and country I ever fled to. *If it weren't for your granda, and what he did to us, maybe I wouldn't have failed you and the baby…and Leslie.* Then, excusing herself, she pulled herself up on her walking frame and took herself to bed.

The night she was born, they took her away to the nursery. I lay there and wondered about Leslie. I pictured him – sorting pots on a big fishing boat, throwing the ones he didn't want overboard, finishing work and walking around Geraldton, alone, missing me and not even knowing for sure if he was a dad. I thought maybe I could go up there on the bus with the baby. I'd explain to him the story I had invented, of the stranger at the train station who'd looked a bit like Elvis Presley. I fell asleep, waking a short while later to the sound of whispering. Opening my eyes to a slit, I peeked across the room. Gran and the matron sat together. Matron covered my gran's hand with hers. I closed my eyes and pretended to sleep while Gran wept. Until I got myself pregnant to that stranger I'd just met, and shamed her, I'd never seen her cry like that. Not when my mum dumped me and said she wasn't coming back. Not when I told her about Granda dressed in his old army uniform and hanging from the apple tree up the back, just two days before Elvis fell down and died in his own bathroom.

The next night, a nurse came to my bedside. They'd moved me into a tiny corner room tucked out of sight from the main ward. Curled in a ball, my face towards the wall, staring at the emergency bell, I wondered if being sad constituted an emergency. I rolled over to see the nurse standing next to me, the baby in her arms. My breasts charged with milk and tingled as she pressed the baby to my chest. The nurse walked out of the room, leaving her in my arms, her rosebud mouth nuzzling into my nightie, seeking the nourishment I wasn't supposed to allow her.

When the nurse returned to take her away, I wanted to thank her. But nothing came out.

She looked down at the baby I'd privately named Lisa Marie, stroked her tiny forceps-bruised face, and lifted her from my arms.

I doodle around the edges of my boarding pass. Boxed-in houses give way to hearts and flowers with slightly evil grinning faces. I draw a stick man with a cape and an Elvis quiff and snarl. I wonder if Leslie had been happy at any point in his adult life, with all those fish, all those wives and children. I sketch an oversized pedestal for the stick man to stand on. I decide I wouldn't have looked him up and said hello, nonchalantly or otherwise, had he still been alive. It took me thirty-three years to return for good, but my guilt and shame remain too complex. I write *You'd have made a great dad to Lisa-Marie* where a plaque would sit, then scribble it out so that the pen pushes through the paper and stains the computer table with a blue blob. The internet tells me that while I was still in the air earlier today, a leadership spill was called but no-one challenged the Prime Minister. The events, led presumably by Gran's infamous horseless men, overshadowed the national apology. It takes a while to understand the significance of the occasion and to understand why people were upset by the shenanigans in Canberra. I listen over and over again to the clip I link to on the ABC news website. I scan the faces in the crowd, just in case I see her. But of course the Prime Minister isn't speaking to me. I wasn't actually forced to do anything, and though I have never stopped looking, according to the records I tracked down in the mid-nineties my baby died when she was six months old, before I even started running.

They came with the papers on the final morning. Face to the wall, I reached behind me for her hand, but Gran had already left the room. The matron stood beside me, one hand on my shoulder. *Yes, father unknown*, I confirmed.

It's best this way…for all concerned, she'd said pointedly.

I refused to look up as I reached for the pen. Printing my name in tight letters, I drew a tiny heart where the dot above the 'i' belonged. I cried and didn't care if I shattered into a thousand shards.

I rolled over and saw a brittle woman in a beige suit take the papers from Matron and shove them into a briefcase, locking it before nodding at me. I said I needed to speak to someone, that it was important, and began to sit up. But the tight-faced woman had gone with my signed paper in her briefcase, and Gran was outside, waiting to take me back home and tuck me up on the good couch in the lounge room with my old Holly Hobbie bedspread. Waiting to kiss me and say, *You and me, we're all we've got now*, before she had to go off again and feed faces and wipe bums.

Gran calls out my name. *Do you need more blankets?* She says there is Horlicks in the cupboard. She hasn't been asleep, after all. I recall those few months I worked alongside her in the nursing home, the more lucid of the elderly claiming not to sleep, ever. I tell her I am fine, that I am going to bed now. I stand by her door and add that I am glad to be home. Pressing the button on my phone to light up the screen, I peek in at her. *Goodnight, Gran.*

I didn't look as the officious woman and a nurse wheeled Lisa Marie down the corridor and away for the last time, but I could sense the gap stretching between us; sensed her disappearing further and further from my reach. One of the wheels on the plastic hospital bassinet squeaked thirty-three times, each more quietly than the last, until I couldn't count anymore.

2016

Can of worms

'You wouldn't believe how many Poms sang *that* one while I was behind the bar. Vegemite and chunder, and the songs those *Neighbours* kids released. That's about the extent of the Australian music I heard.'

He's passing another tray to me as I say that. I shift position to reach for the seedlings and my knee grinds.

'And the chunder song had been out for years before I left. No imagination, those punters.'

'Only Kylie and Jason?' David sounds incredulous. 'You need educating. You've missed over twenty years of music.'

He asks if I want to rest for a bit. Reaching for my hand, he helps me up and says he's got a couple of beers stashed in the cooler bag in the back of his ute, that this place has been stripped of vegetation for decades and a few more minutes is hardly going to make a difference.

As we down tools and walk away, a couple of the group give us a look of self-righteousness – or maybe jealousy of the fact that we appear to be shooting through.

Just two weeks earlier, at Gran's wake, David's son Graeme had shown up, looking for his dad, and a short while later bailed up the two of us in a corner of the town hall to rant in that passionate way only the under twenty-fives seem to be able to get away with. *Grass and trees, that is what you people took from the land. Salt — that's your legacy.*

Peering around the room as subtly as I could manage, trying to see who else he'd reached, I was struck by the rainbow of colours scattered among the darker, more typical attire worn for an old lady's funeral — striped woollen tights, brightly knitted vests, strange beanies that Wee Willie Winkie himself may have donated to the op shop. All afternoon, along with wishing Gran were here to witness this rather bizarre community event so that she could put her acerbic slant on the retelling, I'd felt slightly affronted by what I perceived as a lack of decorum, and wondered if Gran was right, that I'd become straitlaced in all those years away.

As far as I could tell, nobody else had heard Graeme's rant. It appeared that there were few people older than David and me in the room. Nobody who could be held directly responsible for the degradation of forested land decades earlier, at any rate. Instead, there were mostly first-generation tree-changers, societal dropouts and upwardly mobile tradesmen with their wives — people I'd met, but had not formed a bond with since returning.

Gran called anyone who'd been in the district for less time than she had 'the Newcomers'. By the time she died, under those terms, that meant more or less everyone. In the letters and emails she'd sent while I was overseas, it had seemed she was most entertained by the dropouts from mainstream society — the forty-years-too-late hippies — those who'd thrown in corporate and other lives. They'd been attracted to the town, she'd said, by the promise of being welcomed for all their differences from the mainstream thinkers. When she'd worked at the general store, they'd gone to great pains to mention those differences when trying to extract information from Gran — one of the *last of the old-timers* — about days past.

Over time, Gran had reported, they'd enriched the district, establishing businesses to revitalise the town — a food co-op, handmade and recycled clothing boutiques so they could look different together in the same way, hairstylists, piercing salons, quiet places to practise whichever Eastern spirituality was the flavour of the month, arty-crafty spaces that taught skills designed to enable everyone to be an artist, a musician, a photographer, or a dancer to the beat of his or her own drum. Before long, a group had opened an alternative school promoting educational opportunities for non-mainstream thinkers. Telling me that story one day as we sat people-watching in the town square of the last Spanish village I'd tried to make my home, she'd laughed and spilled her sangria into her lap as she said that over the past fifteen years, they'd escaped one mainstream only to create a whole new mainstream here.

She'd been delighted as, later, other families began moving into the district – tree-changers searching for simplicity. But not long after arriving here, they'd found life perhaps a little too simple, so they'd modernised and extended the houses they'd purchased, and sometimes reopened old businesses. The newsagent changed hands, a childcare centre opened, and a doctor and pharmacist moved in, after years of the town being without either. Gran wrote newsy emails saying that she'd been surprised, at first, to discover that the men would leave their families to fend for themselves while they worked away on the mines for a month at a time. *It's a town of mothers and children once more. It's as if the men are all off at war again.* A few months later, she'd decided that although the fathers were often only there part-time, the influx had been good for the town. The local school had expanded, the supermarket had reopened, and even the old people's home where she'd worked had grown hopeful of attracting new residents in the future.

When she'd started to sell me the idea of my returning home, I had anticipated and imagined these changes. But though her letters and emails were rich, and the stories she told me on her yearly visits complexly woven with the minutiae of her daily life, upon arriving back here I'd initially felt as though I had landed in an alien country.

As I have discovered since returning, there are myriad competing environmental 'care' and 'resuscitation' groups established by the

Newcomers. In town for his mid-semester university break, Graeme had begun outlining the benefits of his favourite group – and I found myself volunteering to go with him two weeks later.

This district was founded by men with big dreams revolving around the removal of trees from the landscape. Graeme's dream was to replant the district, one paddock at a time. As he outlined the schedule for the day, I was struck by the fact that, standing there with his big woolly beard, so disproportionate to his slightly owlish nineteen-year-old face, wearing his thick-framed glasses and designer-label flannel shirt, Graeme looked more like a cartoonish representation of a lumberjack than any of the region's timber-chopping forebears. I'd started laughing raucously at my own thoughts, and poor David had looked appalled that his son had set me off. *Settle down, mate,* David said to him. *Bit of sensitivity. Louise's just lost her grandmother.*

My legs stretched and my back straightened, I feel liberated when we reach David's car, parked under the shade of the sole karri tree in the entire area. Among the cars belonging to the conservation group are a number of bicycles, including several shiny new ones, designed to look old-fashioned, with bulky frames and lacking gears.

'Stupid bloody kids,' he says. 'Nostalgic for the past. Don't they know they invented gears and engines for a reason? It's too late for the planet, anyway. Replanting a bit of lovegrass isn't going to save us.'

I tell him that I had thought that an organic farmer would be at least a little optimistic about the future. 'Maybe they should rename it, something more powerful, perhaps,' I add. 'Lovegrass sounds like a Kylie song.'

Graeme, having guilt-tripped us into coming out here to plant, is conspicuously absent. *A big night with the local boys.* David had shrugged apologetically after turning up alone to pick me up at that ridiculous hour this morning. *What can I say? Underneath he's a city boy with a city boy's constitution.* He'd told me at Gran's funeral that Graeme had been raised in the suburbs, had not even started visiting this place until five years earlier, when his parents had separated and David came back to the family property.

I lean against the ute tray and yawn. My body clock still has not readjusted to country ways of early to bed, early to rise. Instead, late into the night I roam the world via Google and Google Earth, revisiting all those places I tried to bend and mould myself into over the years I was away. I know more about the population of those cities and villages, the lifestyles of the locals, the industry and even the celebrity culture, than I ever knew while there.

'Are we the only ones left now?' I ask, reaching for the beer.

In the past months, there has been a run of funerals of elderly people, and streams of strange but vaguely familiar faces coming to town for several days before disappearing for what I expect will be the last time. I don't think there is anyone at all left from Gran's generation, and it seems all of those old enough to be of our parents' generation took off or have died.

'Maybe we're it,' I chuckle. 'Two fifty-somethings who nearly got away – then moved back home when we failed at grown-up life.'

'Get fucked,' he says. But he's laughing.

I'm hoping he'll offer to drop me home now. I really don't want to return to planting grass. 'Surely there's something else we can do to earn karma points from the planet?'

I'd tried to wangle my way out of coming when Graeme hadn't shown up with his father. I was nervous about spending the day with a bunch of strangers, didn't want to have to deal with the compassionate words and uninvited hugs that seem to be the order of the day when someone around here dies. David had refused to come without me, saying it might get my mind off things, and that I might enjoy getting involved in the community. *Help you reconnect*, he'd said, disregarding my claim that I'd never felt connected in the first place.

I hated this town. Why do you think I left at seventeen? I'd said. *Just let me go back inside and you go play at extreme planet-saving.*

He wasn't the only one ever to disregard such assertions. Gran had never given up on trying to coerce me into coming back where I 'belonged'. And Raimond had said at least several times throughout that last year we were together that I needed to come back. *You have a longing, a nostalgia for a return to the home.* I'd denied it, telling myself it was only that he was desperate to return to his crazy ex, and it would be easier with me out of the picture. And there was the story I'd told myself for my entire adult life: that the town itself was somehow toxic to me.

David reaches in and grabs the bottle of sunscreen from the floor of the car and passes it to me, picking up the conversation where we'd left off earlier. 'Thought our music was huge over there – Hutchence, Cave, Accadacca. I used to watch those stadium shows on the box and sometimes I thought of you there. Jealous as buggery, I was.'

He lights a cigarette and I put my hand over my nose, pretending to scratch my face.

'Maybe you should get one of those vaping thingummies that your hip young son uses. Did you just say you were *jealous* – of me?'

'We all were. You were the first to leave the town – the state, the country. Made our lives look pretty ordinary.'

If I knew him better, maybe I'd tell him the truth of the matter – that my constant shame and misery overrode most of the good while I was away. That I'd felt compelled to punish myself. That for some inexplicable reason, I needed to feel closed in and claustrophobic in those cities and villages under the northern hemisphere skies.

'You got away,' I say. Then, without meaning to, I add, 'I wasn't the first to leave. Leslie was.'

He looks directly at me. 'How about that bloody statue, eh?' The corners of his mouth turn up and he's got a glint in his eye. 'Bet nobody erects a fucking ugly statue when *we* cark it.'

While we finish our beers, we reminisce about the bizarre unveiling ceremony held on the first anniversary of Leslie's death. An ABC team rolled into town, and some of Leslie's siblings had shown up, along with his older children. It had been painfully confronting to see them, younger female versions of him, but already close to twice the age he'd been when we'd parted ways. Mostly, though, it was all the Newcomers, thrilled, it seemed, to be a part of something that would anchor them to the town. At best, Gran had said, a few of them may have met Leslie on his infrequent trips back. It had been years since he'd been here, though, and she suspected that nobody had a clue about him beyond the facts that he'd grown up in the town, and had established the biggest fishing fleet in the state.

I'd wanted to stay away. Gran's health was declining rapidly, but she'd insisted on going along. That meant I was compelled to go, too. As David and I had stood either side of Gran's chair at the back of the crowd, alongside Leslie's siblings and children, he had kept reaching behind the chair and nudging me as various local public figures got up to speak about Leslie. We'd avoided making eye contact lest we laugh out loud at the ridiculousness of the occasion. The stranger Leslie had saved from the jaws of the shark stood to speak, and the Newcomers went wild at the scripted speech and unveiling of the apparently artistic representation of their new local hero. Then, when the ABC reporter, a young woman of perhaps nineteen, sought people to interview from the crowd, she'd homed in on the best-looking men. Stuck up in the back, none of us who'd known him got so much as a look-in.

'C'mon. Fuck this. Let's go,' David says, throwing his empty stubby into the ute tray. He opens the car door and practically shoves me in. 'I want to take you somewhere.'

Two weeks earlier, the night of Gran's funeral, I'd been disturbed by heavy rapping on the front door. Dragging myself out of the shower, throwing on Gran's old chenille gown and sliding my feet into my manky ugg boots, I'd shuffled down the hallway and opened the door, to find David on the doorstep. He was still wearing the ill-fitting suit he'd worn to the service, albeit with the top few shirt buttons undone and the tie unknotted and draped like a scarf. He held a bottle of wine in one hand and a pizza box in the other, and passed them to me like precious offerings while I stood dumbly with my hand on the doorknob.

Hungry?

Smelling the yeasty dough, the pepperoni and melted cheese, I realised that I was starving, but I wasn't sure that I wanted his, or anyone's, company.

When he'd walked into the funeral home earlier in the day, it was only the fourth or fifth time I'd seen him since returning to live with Gran. He'd come up to me when I was surrounded and placed his arms across my shoulder in a matey fashion, avoiding the overfamiliarity that others were showing towards me. I appreciated that, and found myself gravitating towards him when the hugging and kindly words about my *living treasure, the town matriarch* and *universally beloved* grandmother grew too much.

The first time I saw David after coming back, I'd been standing behind him in line at the newsagent's, waiting to do Gran's lotto. He'd turned around and done a double take, before commenting on my unruly hair. In all my years away, I'd somehow forgotten about the propensity of rural men either to say nothing at all or to let loose with whatever often-uncensored verbiage bled from their mouths. Returning to my hometown after years away, I'd felt every one of my fifty years. Yet in those first months, whenever I moved about the town, it seemed as though the decades of absence faded. And while everything looked and felt changed, I had to work to resist responding to my surroundings as I might have done as an angry and shamed teenager. Logically, I knew that nobody really knew me, but I couldn't quite shake the sense that behind my back everyone was whispering about me. I decided not to respond to the odd man in the line. My hair – unruly or otherwise – was not a topic for discussion with a stranger.

Five minutes later, as I was about to pull out of the parking bay in the main street, he called me by name and asked if I'd forgotten him. Immediately defensive, I looked him over – according to him, as if he were a bull at an auction that I may or may not have an interest in bidding on. It had been more than thirty years since I left my grandmother's house and the town. I had no idea who he might be. But when he made the bull-at-auction comment, I relaxed and replied that I was sorry, that I hadn't known any grey-haired paunchy men other than old Johnno when I left, and *he* was a long time dead. Then he reminded me that we'd been house captains at primary school – and that in our brief period of friendship as troubled teenagers, I'd once thrown up all over him after sculling his can of bourbon and Coke.

That encounter in the parking bay set the tone for subsequent meetings.

Half an hour after absconding from revegetation duties, we're passing the old abattoir on the creek bank and I'm startled to discover that there's a luxury sheepskin products store built around the ruins of the old building. I wonder to myself if David ever spent time out there among the bones of the abattoir as a teen; whether, like me, he had felt somehow comforted in the presence of the ghosts of all those animals. Although I've thought about those days often, in several years back in the town I haven't come out this way. Most of the places of my childhood have distorted in my mind, and when re-encountering them on my return, I had been challenged by the fact that everything had seemed familiar, yet smaller, faded, and less significant than I remembered it. The creek, though, looks deeper and more flowing than I recollect, and on its banks I note brightly painted picnic tables with contrasting Colorbond shades constructed over them. As kids we'd come out here and play in the scrub, make cubbies out of old car bodies and dumped fridges. Now, in that same place, there is lawn of an odd, luminous shade of green that you might see on an over-fertilised golf course. The effect is slightly surreal, akin to that of the somewhat eccentric Wes Anderson movie I'd watched on DVD a few days earlier.

'I wonder how they define a *luxury sheepskin product*,' I say, and we amuse ourselves for a few minutes, listing increasingly outlandish and crude possibilities.

'I'm taking you to your farm,' he says after a while. I'd already figured that out, but allow him to think that he's surprised me.

In the short time since Gran's been gone, I've been on a mission to purge excess. I thought that once things settled down, maybe I'd sell up, see another part of the world. I had piles of possessions to go through, and garbage bags of sorted clothes and household items to donate to the op shop already lined the edges of the room.

When David came that night of the funeral, he'd raised his eyebrows. *You're allowed to take your time. I haven't even started on the old man's crap, and it's been a few years.* As his fingers released the bottle, they'd brushed against mine, and for the first time since waking to a too-quiet house and knowing instinctively that Gran had died in her sleep, I cried. *I can help, if you want,* he offered once I stopped.

After I'd devoured most of the pizza and a good slug of the wine, I'd asked him if he'd mind lifting a couple of heavy boxes from a shelf in the walk-in cupboard. I'd tried, but they were unwieldy and heavy. I could not, for the life of me, imagine how Gran might have got them up there, over a metre off the ground. After showing him the two boxes, I'd looked down and, realising what I was wearing, excused myself to get changed.

I came back in wearing an only slightly more presentable windcheater and pair of trackpants. He'd turned, holding a small wooden box that had been pushed into the far corner behind the larger ones he'd retrieved for me.

I had no recollection of ever seeing it before. *Must be something of Gran's*, I said, blowing a fine layer of dust from the top. I noted the green satin bow, looped into a double knot, at the top of the box and remembered the camphor chest filled with linen and soft woollen winter blankets that Gran used to have at the foot of her bed back on the farm. I recalled the plastic bag of fabric scraps, ribbons and skeins of wool that had been kept in there, too. They'd been my mother's, left over from when Gran had been teaching her to knit and sew. And when Gran was preoccupied with working outside or dealing with Granda, sometimes I'd creep into her room, pull the bag out and try to imagine my mother as a little girl, making dresses for her dolls.

Maybe I should put it back. I hoped that I sounded as though I was making light of his find. *Might be a can of worms.* I gave the box a little shake. Nothing rattled or clunked. It didn't weigh much. *Can you put it back for me?* I'd asked, though I was perfectly capable of doing it for myself. *It must be my mother's and I'm not sure that I can deal with opening Pandora's box today, of all days.*

It's been nearly forty years since Gran drove us out of here with the back of Granda's clapped-out green ute piled up. *We're making a clean start*, she'd said, refusing to let me be sentimental. *They're just things, Louise*, she'd snapped, as I stood by the car and stared at most of our furniture, the contents of Granda's sheds, and even his clothes, dragged outside and thrown into heaps about the yard for our neighbour Callum Rowley to collect in his truck and give to the needy. I'd imagined all of our possessions reappearing in the future, being worn by the poor people, sat and slept on by the needy, and appropriated by the unscrupulous.

Sometimes, even now, with the rebranded and named op shop as *The Place for Vintage Collectables* being so trendy, I half expect to find the worldly possessions of three generations of Kellys sitting on the shop floor, or to be confronted by someone wearing Granda's clothes, or his false foot, in the main street.

We're travelling light, without excess, into our future. Gran had been rough as she uncurled my hands from their position, gripped around the open car doorframe, and shoved me into the passenger seat.

Sitting in another passenger seat now, travelling up the overgrown and neglected track that used to be the annually graded driveway to my home, I am hyper-aware of my surroundings. David concentrates on manoeuvring around the largest of the potholes and nods and grunts at my increasing chatter. I say that I could fall asleep anywhere in the world, but if I woke here, I'd know it as though I know my own face. Then I laugh, perhaps a touch artificially, and say that I actually try to avoid seeing my face as it grows into an old woman's.

'I can turn back,' he says, after a few minutes pass and I've started crying again. 'It is just a bit of land – thought it might cheer you up.'

There is one more bend before we reach where the house used to stand. I wipe my eyes and nose with the sleeve of my windcheater.

'You're nice,' I say.

He groans and turns to me. 'Nice?'

'Keep going. I'm not crying about coming here,' I say as we round the final bend.

A decade or so after I left Australia, the house burned down. Gran reported it to me in her tiny scrawling writing in one of the blue aerogram letters she sent before the internet came along to simplify and depersonalise keeping in touch. She'd gone out there afterwards, she'd said, for one last look, but nothing of her old life had remained. At the time, I'd felt a flush of anger at her. After moving us to the town's outskirts, she'd made me promise never to return to the farm.

David pulls the car over and stops near a crumbling stone chimney, all that remains of the old farmhouse.

'Okay? Want to get out?'

I nod and open the car door.

'C'mon,' he says. 'Let's walk up the hill.'

At the top, we sit looking down at the area that once contained my home, the farmhouse and all the outbuildings. I used to come up here with Leslie, and spy on Gran and Granda with Granda's binoculars.

'See over there.' I point to a green spot in the distance. 'That was the Rowleys' place. My mum told me about her baby brother, walking all that way and falling into their dam. She didn't believe it, said that when she was little she believed a bad man came and took him there.'

I don't say that after my mother sent me back to live with Gran and Granda for the final time, we came up here to watch for kidnappers and murderers.

'You know they said your gran came out here and did it, don't you?'

'What? Drowned her own baby? Well, *they'd* be wrong. She wasn't even there.'

'The fire. Talk about the town was she did it. Nothing ever came of it, though. Fucken small towns, huh?'

I remember, then, how in those weeks before we left the farm, Gran had been filled with rage. I cannot imagine, now, the strength it must have taken to drag all of the heavy furniture out of the house and the tools from the shed, to haul it all across the yard and pile it up like that.

'I came outside one night after being woken by sounds,' I say, 'and she was trying to chop down the apple tree with an axe. Can you imagine that?'

I'd watched her for a while, from the back step. She wore only her long flannelette nightie, and under the moonlight she'd appeared ghostly. I was mesmerised but had to keep closing my eyes to try to make the image of Granda, caught in the apple tree – or so I'd thought, at first, after discovering him – disappear.

We sit without speaking. He passes me his water bottle and asks if I remember what I'd told him before going away.

'Of course, I remember. I'd hardly forget that.'

I'd left town the day after telling him about my baby, of signing her life away. And of counting the squeaks as they'd wheeled her hospital bassinet away. *Leslie*, he'd said. It was more statement than question, but I'd refused to answer him.

'He knew,' David says after a while. 'Leslie. The last time he was here with his family, long after you'd left the country. Sorry. Thought you should know that I told him.'

After David went home the night of Gran's service, I'd tried to sleep. Eventually, I got up and went to the cupboard and took the box into the kitchen. I sat for a long time, hours perhaps, before cutting the ribbon and prising the box lid open. Inside were newspaper clippings about the disappearance of a toddler – my uncle – a bundle of letters tied with string, a tatty rag, several small toys and trinkets. Rifling through and reaching the bottom of the box, I'd found an envelope addressed to me. I realised that this was Gran's box, not my mother's.

I'd included Gran's address with all the queries I'd begun sending out from the time Lisa Marie would have been almost eighteen. I told Gran I was doing it, and asked her to let me know of any information that came back. The day I'd opened Gran's aerogram, all those years ago, I'd had a feeling it would be the day that I would find out something, something concrete. I'd indulged in a fantasy – a reunion – Lisa Marie, Leslie and me. I hadn't expected to read that Lisa Marie had died when she was just a baby.

'It *is* just a place, isn't it?' I stretch my arms wide. 'This. It isn't home. Not now...' I drop my arms and look down. 'It turns out she died very young – cot death.'

Reaching into my pocket, I pull out the envelope I've been carrying since I found it. The last person to handle it had placed a small dab of glue on the seal. I show it to him and tell him it was in the box, that I'd already compared it with the letters from inside the box that my mother had written to Gran throughout her years of absence.

'It isn't her writing,' I say. 'Nor my gran's.'

I'd suspected all along that Gran had not been quite honest with me – about many things – and that she'd had her reasons for keeping secrets. My hand shakes as I hand it to him and ask him to open the resealed letter. I tell him to read it to himself first, and then decide whether I need to hear it.

He takes it.

'You sure? It can't be unread. Or unheard.'

Now it's spread out before me, I see that the farm was quite small, perhaps fifty acres or so.

'It's dated 1999,' he says. 'You should read it for yourself.'

'No,' I say. 'I'd prefer my old pal told me what it says.'

He reads the letter and sits without speaking.

I think of that trip Gran had made to see me in 1999. She'd said she had something to tell me, on New Year's Eve, before all the technology got wiped by the millennium bug. She'd told me she'd kept secrets that would change the way I thought of her. I'd brushed her away. I said I didn't want to know her secrets. My mother had already told me, when I was a little girl, that my *precious grandmother* had been in love with old Doc Wilson. *Why do ya think your Granda is like he is?* she'd asked me once, as if at eight I could make meaning from her words. I'd assumed that was what Gran had wanted to tell me. *You're my grandmother. Your secrets are not for me*, I'd said to her, just before the clock struck midnight.

But they were for me to know, those secrets. She'd all but admitted it when I came home, hadn't she. She'd let me down, she'd said. And the baby and Leslie, too.

'She knew all along who took the baby, didn't she?'

He nods. 'Looks like it.'

I clasp my hands together.

'But this letter, Lou?' he says. 'It was written by her – the baby.'

ACKNOWLEDGEMENTS

This book is a work of imagination. Yes, a man in Wales once served me a weird meal consisting of baked beans stuffed into a potato, topped it with yellow cheese, and gave it a fancy name. And an Australian prime minister apologised for the horrors of the past while people worked against her in the background. Elvis Presley once talked to me via a ouija board, too. But while some actual people and events are referred to, the characters of these stories are not consciously or purposefully based on anyone I've known, living or otherwise.

For helping to bring the stories forth I'm indebted to my friends scattered around the country and the globe, who've shared lives and experiences, answered my nosy questions, boosted my confidence and tolerated me banging on endlessly about life, books and writing – for decades, in some instances. I'm especially grateful to those who racked their brains to consider what they wore or remembered of rural Australia in a particular year; told me about their years working in a crappy London pub, pretending not to be homesick; reminded me of the lyrics to a cringe-worthy Kylie song; shared wine and compared stories about bad decisions and obsessions; or reminisced over cups of tea. To those who challenged me, posed or answered a question that went on to inform this collection, either directly or indirectly, I thank you. You make life interesting.

I am hugely grateful to the passionate and dedicated team at UWA Publishing. You have all been consistently professional and dedicated throughout the process of bringing my work to publication. I am especially indebted to Terri-ann White, for many years of support and encouragement of my

ACKNOWLEDGEMENTS

writing. Your enthusiasm for this project has been uplifting, and I feel honoured to have been invited to publish with your fabulous team.

Amanda Curtin, your generosity to fellow writers is humbling. Your editorial signposts are perceptive, and your dedication and attention to detail, astounding. Thanks to you, the reader has been spared from my worst writing excesses and sins, and I think I may have finally banished the inappropriately used em-dash from my bag of tricks.

Thanks too, to Alissa Dinallo for the cover design that wraps my words so beautifully.

An earlier version of 'Leaving Elvis' won the *Australian Book Review* 2013 Elizabeth Jolley Short Story Prize, and was published in *ABR* in October of the same year. I am most appreciative of the support of Peter Rose, and everyone involved with *ABR* and the competition. I feel privileged to have won the prize and am certain that this collection would not have evolved in quite the same way – or perhaps at all – had I not had been shortlisted alongside two outstanding writers. Similarly, 'Happy Haven Holiday Park' was published in *Westerly*, November 2014. I am grateful for the opportunity afforded by Delys Bird, then editor, in inviting me to submit a story to the journal.

Alison Manning, having you on my team has ensured that for the past eighteen months or so my writing life has been rich in ways I had never imagined possible. Likewise, to my RWCs, without you this period would have been more angsty, less rewarding, and there'd have been fewer laughs.

Luke Davies, it has been a long time coming, but finally here is small recognition for your vote of confidence at a time it was dearly needed. A lot of life has happened in the years since we worked together, but at last a finished book, with a hint of the essence of that mentoring project. Your support continues to mean a great deal to me. My gratitude, too, for kindly allowing me to reproduce the lines from 'Totem'.

Though this was not the book I worked on there, I am indebted to everyone at Varuna – the Writers' House. The fabulous staff and the new writing friends made during my stays over the past few years have enriched my personal and professional life hugely.

Snippets and ideas from a project written in my university Honours year have reappeared in several of these stories. Deborah Robertson and Simone Lazaroo, I remember each of you telling me at different times that

ACKNOWLEDGEMENTS

the ideas that matter never go away. It seems they didn't. Cate Kennedy, thank you for rejecting an early version of what eventually became the story 'Leaving Elvis'. You were supposed to love it; I'm glad, now, that you didn't. Your rejection is my favourite thus far. Kim Scott, I'm grateful to you for writing *True Country* when you did. It wasn't written for me, but it made a difference. You know how, and why. I am indebted, too, to every Australian writer who has shared their words, and fed my insatiable appetite for homegrown literature.

To my family, I am most grateful for the unconditional love and support – to Richard, for always believing my writing mattered, and for other reasons too many and soppy to list. And to Stacey, Alex and Jordan, for staying true to yourselves, and for not asking too many times if I was writing about you. Clearly I didn't…this time.

CPSIA information can be obtained
at www.ICGtesting.com
Printed in the USA
LVHW090834140819
627493LV00008B/624/P